RAVES FOR
THE SEAFARER'S KISS

"A beautiful Norse retelling of *The Little Mermaid*, featuring a young mermaid desperate to break free and a shieldmaiden bent on revenge—dark and romantic, and definitely recommended."

—Laura Lam, author of *Pantomime and False Hearts*

"Dive deep into the dark and brutal waters of the northern sea in this lush, original retelling of *The Little Mermaid*. *The Seafarer's Kiss* took my breath away."

—Heidi Heilig, author of *The Girl from Everywhere*

"… there is plenty of action (spiced up with romance) to keep pages turning"

—*Kirkus Reviews*

The Seafarer's Kiss

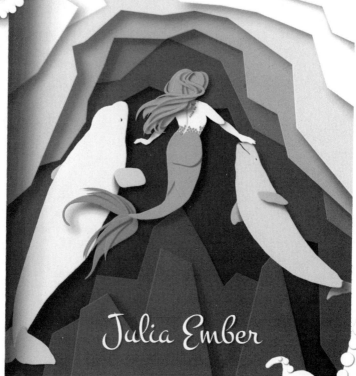

Julia Ember

interlude ⚹ press • new york

For my mom

Part 1: God of Lies

*The trickster god takes many shapes, but they
are without voice. Voices they must steal,
or remain creatures of silence, powerless
without their silver-coated words.*

ICE TABLET A21

*"On all the ships the sails were reefed and there was
fear and trembling. But quietly she sat there,
upon her drifting iceberg, and watched the
blue forked lightning strike the sea."*

—Hans Christian Andersen, *The Little Mermaid*

One

THE AMETHYST DAGGER CALLED TO me from inside the drowned man's chest. The purple hilt gleamed in the light filtering through the rotted floorboards of the ship's deck. Careful not to disturb the bones, I slipped my hand through the skeleton's exposed ribs and pulled the dagger out. It was a prize indeed, different from anything I had in my collection. The blade's edge was still sharp, despite years at the bottom of the ocean.

I could already imagine how the dagger would look glittering beside the helmet and breastplate that I kept behind my table. All my life, I'd collected contraband from these sunken ships: delicate jewels of pearl and gold, bronze statues of animals that roamed the lands far away, a shield engraved with flying creatures that looked like manta rays coasting through the skies. I hid the illegal trinkets in my room and treasured them.

Dodging rusted nails and jagged planks of ancient wood, I swam up through the ship's broken hull. The sunlight above was already fading; midwinter days were over in a matter of hours. I'd wanted to explore the rest of the wreck, to see what other treasures decay had unveiled since my last visit. But if I didn't hurry back,

I'd miss the noon meal, and, this close to The Grading, the king was sure to notice my absence. If we didn't eat, weren't seen to prepare, then he'd want to know why.

Tucking the dagger into my satchel, I swam for home.

When I reached our ice mountain fortress, the hallways were already empty as the rest of the merfolk inside congregated for the meal. I slipped into the great hall unnoticed and took a clamshell tray from the matron who supervised the food line.

I helped myself to a portion of shark fin and a few sand crab legs, covered in a light dusting of brine, and found a quiet space at the end of one of the long ice tables. If I ate quickly, I might have an hour to explore before the sea went black.

I caught the flash of Havamal's silver scales from the corner of my eye. Scowling, I tossed my half-eaten shark fin onto my plate and then reached under the table to retrieve my satchel. A pair of chattering seals had woken me before dawn, and I was in no mood to talk to my former best friend today, not when I had things to do and a ship I wanted to get back to. But before I could I swim away, Havamal put his tray down and scooted along the ice bench to sit beside me.

I growled under my breath. Havamal studied my plate, and then reached over. "Oh, shark fin. They were out by the time I got here. You going to eat that?"

"Help yourself. I was just about to go."

"Oh, come on. I just got here." He sank his teeth into the gnawed fin. Across the table, Vigdis and a handful of other mermaids giggled. Havamal gave them his most charming smile, and I fought the urge to be sick. He was always putting on a show. Then, his blue-gray eyes more solemn, he turned to me and tried to lay a hand on my shoulder. "Come on, Erie, you can't stay mad at me forever."

I stiffened. Before he'd betrayed all our plans by joining the King's Guard, we had been inseparable. I couldn't forgive what he'd done. After all the years we'd been friends, Havamal should know me well enough to understand that.

But as I moved to pull away from him, I was thrown backward into the table by a sudden impact. Havamal reached for me as the floors of our ice fortress shook. A beam of yellow sunlight, brighter than any jellyfish, burst through a network of cracks across the ice of the vaulted ceiling. He tugged me out of the way as Odin's bust shattered above us and sharp blades of ice plunged into the water. Fingers shaking, I reached for his hand. My heart beat so hard all the blood rushed to my ears.

We all pivoted in our seats, looking to the king for answers. Pulling his whalebone trident from behind his throne, King Calder swam down from his frozen crystal dais. He glanced around the room, then motioned a trio of red-tailed guards toward him. With a sigh, Havamal squeezed my fingers, then released my hand. He adjusted the mother-of-pearl harpoon on his shoulder, then leaned over to whisper, "Stay here until we confirm that it's safe."

He swam to the king and took his place among the other guards. I wanted to bristle—I had just as much right to know what was going on as he did—but my heart still pounded against my ribs. I wrapped my arms around my shaking chest.

Havamal's cousin Sila tucked her lilac hair behind her ears and shrugged. "I'm sure it's nothing. A lightning bolt, maybe. It could be the start of the spring storms."

"It's broad daylight." I gestured up toward the sunlight pouring in through our fractured roof. I didn't have a lot of patience for Sila or her stupidity, though she wasn't the worst of Vigdis's crowd. "Do you see any lightning or any rain?"

"Maybe an ice bear?" Sila bit her lip.

"That would have to be one enormous bear." Vigdis snorted and rolled her coral eyes. "To crack the glacier? It's an iceberg. Maybe a blue whale."

Neither of those explanations made sense either. We hadn't had a storm in weeks, so the water was calm and the bergs bobbed in place. Spring could be months away. Though the tide was low enough to drop the water level in the hall to the top of the king's throne, the sea kept its frozen edge. Whatever had caused this quake had to be heavy and traveling fast.

"Maybe humans," I whispered, and the other mermaids went silent. A little jolt of electricity passed through me, like the shock from a jellyfish. A traveling ship could hit the ice mountain with enough force to crack it.

Few humans dared to sail between the treacherous icebergs of our northern waters. The past few years had been some of the coldest we'd ever known, and the floating death traps littered the sea. I'd never seen a human alive before. I only knew what the creatures looked like in death, when water had bloated their pale flesh and sea crabs had picked meat from their skulls, or after the harsh sea currents had stripped them to salt and bone. But some of our legends—those written on the ice tablets King Calder kept locked away now—said that the humans were as beautiful as the gods. I wasn't sure I believed that. Their corpses always looked scrawny with ugly, bare skins. But if humans sailed above us now, I intended to find out.

I pushed back from the table.

"Ersel," Mama hissed from the other end of the long ice bench. Her face was beluga-white, and she clutched the edge of the table. "What are you doing? Don't you dare—"

I might never get another chance like this. Before my mother or the king's remaining guards could stop me, I dove through the archway and out of the hall. Swimming as fast I could, I darted down the network of tunnels and ice caves that wound like sea worm burrows through the glacier's heart. My tail pumped so hard I thought my gills might burst. Only after I reached my own chamber, right at the edge of the fortress, did I chance a look over my shoulder. Nobody followed. I wasn't really surprised. The King's Guard were already few in number, and one still-untested mermaid wasn't worth chasing.

Gulping seawater to calm my breathing, I looked out into the ocean. Mama always cursed our luck. We'd drawn one of the most exposed caves in the year's selection, but I loved how my room opened straight into the grayscale winter sea. From my resting shelf, I could watch the seals dive for fish and hear the belugas trill. I could have chosen to live in the pre-grading caves near the glacier's heart, amongst the other merfolk my own age, but I'd never seen eye to eye with them.

Venturing out through my cave's mouth, I pressed my body against the outer wall of the glacier and swam toward the ocean's surface. The water was dark and calm; the sunlight was blocked by a black shadow protruding from the ice. The ship groaned as water burst through the holes in its wooden bottom. My breath caught in my chest, and I forgot my fear as pure excitement took over. Humans. At last, I was going to see live humans.

With a final kick, I reached the hull of the ship. Barnacles and half-frozen algae clung to its weathered bottom. I ran my hands over the wood, memorizing the foreign texture. The dark titan swayed as waves beat against it; its movement was steady and eerily gentle, almost as if the ship breathed.

A boulder of ice the size of an orca broke off the side of the ice mountain and tumbled onto the ship's deck. Above me, the hull creaked and moaned. Dozens of voices began shouting. In words I couldn't understand, the strange accents blurred, growing louder and more desperate. I dodged to the side as another chunk of ice plunged into the sea and treaded water to stay level with the ship. The quiet breathing ceased, and the titan began sinking into the ocean.

Men dove into the sea. They flailed in the water like underweight sea lions; their arms thrashed as they fought their way back to the surface. I swam closer and touched the bare ankle of the closest sailor. His skin was strangely warm against my scales. His legs moved strangely, kicking at odds rather than smoothly and in tandem. At my touch, he looked down, squinting against the cold and salt. His mouth was so red; his cheeks were so flushed and golden. The sailor screamed, and a cloud of air bubbled upward.

I grabbed him around the waist. There were so many things I wanted to ask him about my treasures. No one had seen me rescue him. I could drag this sailor to the safety of the landmass beyond the ice shelf. I could save him. He kicked and struggled against me; one foot collided with my stomach. I winced at the pain and grunted as I continued to tug the sailor toward the surface.

Then someone else took hold of me, dragging me backward by the arm into the deep. I wasn't strong enough to resist. The sailor fought, desperate to keep swimming toward the surface. He slipped from my grasp and struggled in the frigid open water.

"What were you thinking?" Havamal demanded. "You shouldn't be here. And touching that human? What if it has a disease? What if it attacked you?"

Fighting against him like an animal, I twisted in his grip. Talking to him had been a mistake; allowing myself to reach for him had been worse. That slip had made him confident with me again, and I didn't like it. I didn't want his comfort or his protection—not anymore. I clawed and punched to get free while Havamal swore. He had no right to take my chance from me.

Behind us, the sailor convulsed. He kicked frantically in a last effort to reach the air above, but then the color bled from his angular face, and he stopped fighting. How had he run out of air so soon? The only other sky-breathers I knew were the whales, and they could last twenty minutes or more under water. Would the human have made it to the surface if I'd helped him? I shivered, suddenly cold.

Havamal's grip on my arm relaxed as the human gave a final twitch. "Get back to the hall before the king catches you."

I nodded slowly, and he let me go. But as soon as I was free, I punched him in the stomach. He doubled over in pain.

"I just wanted to speak with him," I hissed. "I just wanted to ask him a few questions."

"And where would you have taken him to have your little chat?" Havamal wheezed. A trail of bubbles seeped from his mouth as he tried to regain his breath. Then he straightened and a ghost smile played at his lips, even though I could still see the pain in his eyes. "You think the king wouldn't find out? That's right. You'd just haul around a fully grown human under his nose, and he'd be none the wiser."

His voice dripped with sarcasm, and, in that moment, I hated him even more.

"Would you tell him?" I accused.

"Of course not." He sighed, rubbing at his abdomen, suddenly looking tired. Some of the rage bled out of me. "I'd never. Now please go back to the hall before someone else finds you."

I nodded, though I had no intention of going back to the hall. By now, everyone would be talking about me and about how I'd made a bizarre spectacle of myself yet again. I'd hide in my ice cave until the rest of them forgot I existed.

Havamal squeezed my hand. I tried to ignore the way my chest tightened at his touch. Whatever we'd had was over. I had to keep reminding myself of that. He'd betrayed me the moment he joined the King's Guard. Now he was defending the ruler who wanted to take away everything we'd once planned together. But he flashed me a tiny smile and the loneliness sang inside me, an echo of that secret song we'd once shared. Then he swam upward, through the rain of sinking bodies, toward the amber sun.

*　　*　　*

I CURLED INTO A BALL on my ice shelf, wrapped my tail around me, and buried my face in my fins. The glacier hummed like a great white whale; the murmur of a thousand morning whispers seeped through the cave walls. Light from the dawn illuminated the crystal ceiling, and I could see Mama's outline like an embossed shadow resting in the crevice above me. I swallowed hard, feeling a little bit queasy. I'd expected her to wake me when she returned from the hall. If she'd needed the night to decide what to say to me about my disappearance, it probably wouldn't be good.

Shaking with cold, I crawled from my shelf and studied my tail fins in the brighter light of our antechamber. Overnight, my topaz scales had darkened to midnight blue. My tail looked shriveled, with loose skin forming wrinkles around my flippers. Our scales had to burn blubber reserves to generate heat through the night. By the look of my tail, a northern current had swept through the glacier while I slept. If I waited much longer to visit the sun and recharge, I'd freeze before Mama had the chance to vent her anger.

As I brushed my hair and got ready, I wondered if Havamal had told anyone where he'd found me. Part of me couldn't imagine him missing the chance to report something to the king and worm his way further into our monarch's good graces, but another part hoped he'd meant it when he told me he still wanted to be friends.

I shoved the hairbrush aside and swam from the cave into the purple dawn sea. Sunlight seeped through the water and lit the glacier from all angles. The ice mountain glowed soft blue, and dozens of shadows moved within its semi-opaque walls. The ship had vanished, but I could see where the ice had cracked, leaving someone's resting chamber exposed to the open sea. A curious pair of gray seals wound in and out of the broken wall. They chattered as they played in the kelp curtains and batted a broken bowl between them.

"You didn't go back to the hall." Havamal's drawling voice called as he drifted from the ruined cave, scooting past the pair of seals. He was trying to hide his smile behind his hand. The metallic silver of his scales glittered, brighter than the North Star. I tried not to stare at the heaving muscles that made a coral-like comb on his pale torso.

Edging over to the broken cave, I grabbed a jagged outcrop to steady myself. "I just wanted to sleep. I figured you'd make up some excuse for me if the king asked, seeing as we used to be friends."

His hand dropped, and a scowl replaced the grin. "Stop it, Erie. You keep saying that just to wind me up. We could still be friends. I want us to go back to the way we were."

"You sold out," I muttered. Honestly, sometimes I did say it to get his reaction. His anger was the only confirmation I had that he'd ever cared about me. But knowing that our friendship had been real never made me feel any better. I drifted into the shadows of the cave, feeling self-conscious about how my dim, night-starved scales and scrawny tail must look to him.

Havamal heaved a sigh so deep it was almost a growl. "No, I just learned to accept that we can't change everything. Have you even thought about your grading next week?"

I lifted my chin and glared at him. "I'm not doing it."

He pressed his lips together and shook his head. "You can only put it off for so long, Erie."

The Grading was an annual ceremony. Aegir's court mage visited the glacier and determined the fertility of each mermaid in her nineteenth year. Then the mermen fought over us, like sharks over a seal pup, vying to win the most fertile mermaids as mates.

It was a future I'd never wanted. Once, Havamal and I had dreamed about escaping together. Before King Calder took the throne from his mother, grading had not been mandatory, and mating was not expected as an immediate outcome. But the king was making new laws that challenged everything our society had stood for. No one was brave enough to stand up to him.

Mama sometimes reminisced about the days when the old queen was alive, ruling our glacier with benevolence rather than through fear. The Grading used to be part of a fall celebration, but now it was a prison sentence. Havamal had agreed with me when I ranted and dreamed of seeing the world, of finding the places where the ships came from and the sources of the warm water currents. We'd explored ancient wrecks together and collected treasures from the seabed.

He used to say, "I will follow you anywhere, as long as we can be together."

All that had ended when he joined the King's Guard. I still visited the old ships, but now my dreams were lonely.

"I have to go. My scales…" Giving him an abrupt nod, I pushed off the cave's ledge and propelled myself into the open water without looking back.

I followed the water vibrations and low trills of a beluga pod I knew well. The water magnified their long-range sounds and made them easy to detect. During the long winters, finding a surfacing hole near the ice shelf wasn't always easy. The ice shifted constantly, but the whales always knew where to find the air.

When I reached them, the beluga pod was swimming in lazy corkscrews between the shallower coastal sea bottom and their breathing hole in the ice. The matriarch glided toward me like a blubbery ghost. A deep silver scar, the result of an encounter with an ice bear, framed her eye. She bumped her nose against my open palm in greeting, and I felt guilty that I hadn't brought them any fish from our stores. The belugas always struggled in the deepest part of winter, when the schools of fish dwindled and the pod had to stay close to their surfacing hole. I grasped the whale's dorsal ridge, and she pulled me up toward the sun.

Something thin and sharp darted into the water.

A juvenile whale dove, keening in pain and leaving a trail of blood behind him. The other belugas ducked under the surface. The matriarch hesitated; bubbles escaped from her lips. After a long moment, another group of juveniles rose to breathe. The stick pierced the water again, narrowly missing an ivory tail.

Murmuring to their leader, the whales huddled beneath the surface. They needed air, and the creatures took turns churning the water to keep the ice from freezing over their opening. They couldn't afford to wait long before surfacing again.

The belugas were too peaceful to fight whatever attacked them from above. They feared the white bears that prowled the ice, just waiting to drag them onto land. But I needed the sun almost as badly as they needed the air. I wasn't about to cower beneath the water. The object looked like a harpoon of sorts, not a bear claw. If one of the younger mermen sat on the ice taunting the whales, he was about to get a piece of my mind.

Squinting at the glittery surface, I studied the harpoon. It swirled impatient ripples in the ocean surface now. It had a silvery tip, tapered and serrated like a shark tooth.

My stomach dropped. Our spears had blades made from ice or mother-of-pearl. Only one creature made objects like this one. I recognized the blade from one of the items in my collection of human treasures. Had one of the sailors survived the shipwreck? It seemed unlikely that a fragile human could survive the cold water long enough to swim to the ice shelf without help, and yet... Maybe one of the merboys had taken the harpoon from the ship after it sank. That explanation seemed far more likely.

I swam under the turquoise blue of the shelf and hid just under the surface. Peering through the distorting ripples of ocean water, I studied the creature. Its face was half covered by a thick black mask of fur and frost. Its eyes moved constantly, but the water blurred the movements and I couldn't tell where its gaze rested.

Taking a deep breath to steady myself, I poked my head above the waves. My hair, gone limp and heavy with the air weighing it down, instantly flopped across my face. I pushed it aside and looked at the human through a parted curtain of wet blue locks. Its rippled form came into focus, and, even under the animal furs, I could make out a tapered waist and curves. A female. She stared back at me; her brown eyes widened. Her crystal breath came fast behind her mask. Then, she screamed.

I froze in the water. The high-pitched sound chilled me worse than the cold sea. The human's gaze drifted skyward, as if she prayed to Odin. Her scream grew louder and louder. I laid a hand on the edge of the ice, ready to hoist myself out and try to calm her, but her harpoon whizzed past my ear. I shrank back. The human still howled, but her eyes had taken on a predatory focus.

I grabbed the weapon by the shaft. The tip of the spear grazed my palm, making a shallow cut. I ignored the pain. Easing back into the water, I stopped kicking my fins to stay afloat. My body sank deeper, and I kept my grip on the weapon.

With nothing to grab, the human couldn't steady herself on the slick ice. She let the harpoon go, and I dropped it into the ocean; I hissed as salt water lapped against the wound on my palm. As the weapon sank, the relieved whales rose. Each of them gently brushed my hip as they took a breath, thanking me in their soft, dignified language of touch.

The belugas' leader swam under me and nudged me up over the ice's lip. The sudden weight of my body as the whale pushed me into the air made me groan with exhaustion. The human girl scurried backward. Even though her feet slipped clumsily on the ice, she put distance between us as fast as she could.

I wanted to study her, but glorious sunlight coated my scales. I tilted my head back as the heat seeped into me, making me drunk and dizzy with pleasure. The human watched me silently from twenty feet away. My body gleamed from my head to the tips of my fins; each of my scales glistened like gemstones. I should have been concerned about the human, but the blast of heat inside me blocked fear. As soon as I ate, all would be well again.

When my scales reached their absorption capacity, the fog in my mind started to clear. Usually, I might crawl inland and look for foxes to watch. But today, I didn't dare stray too far from the water. If the human was brave enough to hunt a whale, I didn't want to leave myself too vulnerable. I lay back on the ice and kept my eyes trained on the girl.

I'd never seen a female among the drowned bodies that littered the northern seafloor. How had she survived the shipwreck? She looked so small and fragile compared to the sailor I'd tried to save. How had she made it back to the surface and through the cold water when he could not?

She continued to scoot backward across the ice. My gaze followed her to a makeshift cave of splintered wood and wet furs. She must have saved some things from the ship, which might explain her survival. Crawling inside the shelter, the human braced another harpoon across her knees and squared her shoulders as if daring me to come closer. But the hostility in her posture didn't quite hide the look of wonder in her wide brown eyes.

Two

My fascination with humans was all Havamal's fault. Our mothers had shared a brooding chamber, and then drawn adjoining caves from the selection when we were old enough to leave the glacier's heart. As children, at dawn on the mornings we didn't have lessons, Havamal would swim into the cave Mama and I lived in, excited and whirling like a tiny silver cyclone. He and I were inseparable: friends and coconspirators, rebels and outcasts from the other kids. Together, we combed the seabed looking for crabs to torment or oysters still concealing their pearls. We laughed the days away, throwing rocks at the seabirds and hitching rides on the backs of patient whales.

Once, Havamal crept into our cave at night. Covering my mouth with his hand, he shook me awake. He clutched a pair of struggling, deep-sea jellyfish by the tentacles, and was using them as a light. I didn't even question where he'd found them. Motioning me to follow, he swam through the ice halls and into the ocean. I still remember the chill of fear that coursed through me. The night brought out creatures that weren't our allies, and no one would realize we were gone until morning.

When I hesitated on the ledge leading out into the sea, he rounded on me. "You're not scared, are you?" He grinned, and the gap in his front teeth was made prominent by the eerie light of the jellyfish's glow. We were nine, and he was still losing his baby teeth—something I teased him about mercilessly. "Come on Erie, don't be a baby."

I wrapped my fingers around the glacier's outer wall and shook my head. Beyond the little ring of light given off by the jellies, I could see nothing in the abyss beyond. The open blackness terrified me, but I didn't want Havamal to tease.

Realizing I was actually afraid, Havamal softened. He reached over his shoulder for the blunted practice harpoon he always carried with him. "Don't worry. There's nothing out there. My dad says narwhals are myths meant to keep us in bed."

He took my hand. His fingers were still sticky with fish oil from the salmon we'd had for dinner, but I trusted him, then, and had faith in his toy weapon and his promises. So when he guided me into the black, I followed him through the deep.

Havamal led us through the sea, somehow knowing where to go despite the darkness. "I heard my dad talking about it," he said, keeping his voice low even though we were alone, where only the sea crabs could hear us. "It sank a few days ago, but he was telling my mum about it. He said it was near the shark bay."

"What is?" I wasn't sure I liked the idea of visiting the shark bay at night. The great whites who lived there were tame enough during the day, but what if they couldn't see us clearly? What if the jellyfish made us smell strange? What if they thought we were whale calves? Or worse, seal pups?

Still, I followed; my trust in him and my curiosity were stronger than fear.

Abruptly, he let go of my hand and pointed downward, dangling the jellyfish so that their light fanned out beneath our fins.

A large wooden beam emerged from the deep, growing upward toward the light like a giant stalk of brown kelp. But instead of protruding from the sand, the mast grew out of a structure, a platform littered with objects that glimmered in shades I'd never seen.

Leaving Havamal behind, I swam down inside the structure. My eyes darted over everything as fast as a zebra fish. A wheel caught my eye. I raced toward it, wrapped my fingers around the spokes, and twisted. The ship groaned and shifted in the sand.

"It's brilliant, right?" Havamal asked as he swam up behind me. He bit his lip to hide his toothless smile, but I could see the glimmer of mischief in his eyes.

"It's amazing," I whispered.

Red with an emotion I couldn't read, his face hovered an inch from mine. Then he brushed a kiss across my forehead. "You're amazing."

Before I could react, he tweaked the end of my nose and swam away, laughing. He beckoned me toward the ship's broken-down interior. "Try and catch me, scaredy! Let's see what's inside!"

*　　*　　*

I slipped into the great hall for the midday meal without passing Mama in the labyrinth. That was a relief, since I hadn't seen her since I fled the hall the night before. She usually ate alone during the day, and preferred to weave her nets while the light was strongest.

After collecting my meal of chopped eel with a garnish of powdered crustacean shell—the cooks were going all out after the chaos of yesterday—I sat on a bench, near a group of merfolk my own age but few places away from them, hoping to avoid interaction; the last thing I wanted was for the conversational focus to shift to my dramatic exit from the hall. I just wanted to eat quickly and go check on the human girl.

But almost as soon as I lifted the first morsel of eel to my lips, Vigdis leaned across the table toward me. "Ersel," she said, too loudly. "We've just been talking about you."

I cringed and looked at the ceiling, praying to the carvings of the gods for help. The fissure made by the ship's impact ran across Frigga's forehead and through Aegir's sea serpent eyes, but the portrait of Loki remained untouched. I took that as a sign and prayed to the trickster. Loki specialized in lies, and I didn't plan to tell any of the other merfolk the truth about the human I'd seen.

Vigdis speared a sea urchin with her ice pick. When she spoke, her voice was layered with false sympathy. "Were you sick last night? You left so fast and looked so pale! I know it was frightening, but with The Grading coming up, I do hope you're not unwell."

With Vigdis, everything was about The Grading. Competition flowed through her veins like blood. She got worse the closer it came, and all her friends seemed to have taken on the obsession as well.

"I just needed to lie down," I said. "My stomach felt queasy."

Flipping her coral hair over one shoulder, she popped the urchin into her mouth and rolled it around with her tongue to crack the shell. "If you don't start taking better care of yourself, your follicle count will be nonexistent. After lunch, why don't you come bask in the sun with us?"

That was the thing with Vigdis: She saw me as competition, but still wanted everyone to believe she cared. A few of her friends traded looks, then nodded toward me, sycophantically echoing their leader's sentiments.

"I don't think I'll do The Grading," I stammered. This was why I still chose to stay with Mama. I never knew what to say to defend myself when they all ganged up on me, no matter how pathetic I found them. I couldn't imagine choosing any of them to share my cave.

Vigdis's eyebrows shot up. The sickly sweet tone dropped from her voice, replaced by genuine shock. "How do you expect to find a mate?"

"I'm not sure I want one at all," I said, staring down into my bowl as my cheeks burned. I wasn't sure why I was embarrassed when the choice should have been mine. But I knew that every other nineteen-year-old mermaid would take the test given by Aegir's shadow mage, though, since every older mermaid was bound to silence, none of us knew what went on once the chamber was sealed and the mage began her work.

I wasn't sure the king would let me refuse, but I clung to the hope that I could put it off for just a little while longer, until I could plan my escape. I hated the entire spectacle. Most of us paired off after the ceremony. Our scores were the only things the mermen ever learned from Aegir's mage. The score was the only thing about us that mattered to them, as if everything else that made us who we were meant nothing.

If I found a mate, my days of freedom were over. Everyone would expect me to sit on the eggs until they hatched, day in, day out, waiting for my mate to return with the food he hunted and warm me with his scales. The king's new laws dictated it. He enforced them as the birthrate in our glacier started to fall. He said it was to protect us and make sure that any viable eggs survived into childhood.

But I wasn't ready for confinement, and I definitely wasn't ready for the responsibility that came afterward. I'd heard the horror stories of cruel mermen who kept their mates locked below the ice, where they hatched brood after brood while their bodies withered and their minds broke. I didn't know if all the stories were true, but some girls from years before mine had gone below and I'd never seen them again. People said King Calder was deaf to appeals.

When she recovered herself enough, Vigdis's pixie features smoothed into a grimace of concern. "I know you must be worried. Everyone can see that you're looking a bit... off. I'm sure someone will ask you, but not if you don't come to the ceremony at all."

"I'm not worried!" I burst out. I hated that they all thought I was afraid of failing, when in reality I was much more afraid of success. "I just don't know if I want to have a mate."

"Why not?" Havamal asked softly, sliding down the bench toward us. I almost groaned out loud. I hadn't noticed when he joined us.

"Because she's a silly child who would rather spend her time making pets of the whales than starting a life for herself," Vigdis said, keeping her tone singsong sweet despite the venom in her words. She turned away from me and stroked Havamal's muscular arm; her fingers traced circles over the band of silver scales that wound up his bicep.

I swallowed a morsel of bitterness. It annoyed me that Havamal had grown up to be so good-looking… so irksomely muscular and well-proportioned. The other mermaids fawned over him and hung on his every word. If there was any justice under the sea, he would have remained gap-toothed and gangly for the rest of his life.

Havamal shrugged her off. He focused his hunter's stare on me. "Why, Ersel?"

"Mama does fine alone." It wasn't a real answer, but it was the only one I was prepared to give with all of them staring at me. My mother had only taken one mate in her lifetime. My father had died right after I'd hatched. I didn't have any memories of him.

Vigdis barked a laugh. "Fine? She's lonely. Everyone can see it. She hardly leaves the glacier, and her scales have turned gray. Isn't that why you still live with her? To keep her company?"

"She does seem kind of lonely sometimes," Havamal admitted. "Do you really want that?"

The eels suddenly tasted sour. I didn't want to be here, listening to them talk about Mama. I knew what the others in the glacier said about her. I spat into my palm and pushed back from the table. I needed to get away from Vigdis and her grating fake concern.

"Wait!" Havamal said, reaching for my arm. "Erie, don't be like that—"

I jerked back as if he were a poisonous jelly. "I told you not to touch me."

Hurt flashed across his handsome face, and he pulled his arm back to his chest. How dare he side with Vigdis? I knew what was expected of me. I knew Mama was isolated, shunned even, for failing to take another mate after my father passed. Even the king's law wouldn't force her to mate a second time, but there was law, and then there was what everyone expected. I hated that. I hated all of them.

Without waiting for the king's permission, I swam past the assembled merfolk and out into the ocean.

I WAS SO ANGRY MY thoughts blurred as I swam for the ice shelf as fast as I could. I wanted to get away from all their expectations and do something wild, rebellious—something like visiting a human. My fins cramped as, refusing to stop even to catch my breath, I pushed my body to its limits. As the blind rage subsided, I found myself at the belugas' surfacing hole. I wound in and out of their sea-cloud bodies as I pushed myself up toward the waiting ice. The matriarch let me grasp her fin. The sun was setting above the shelf, and the ice glittered purple.

Releasing the leader's fin, I paddled to the edge of the drift and surfaced. The air above was dry and biting. The wind was sharp with fragments of broken ice, the precursor to a winter storm. Could the human survive that kind of weather? When the storms broke, sometimes even the seals sought refuge underwater. Shading my eyes, I peered out at the barren earth.

The human girl sat twenty paces from the belugas. She was wrapped in so many furs it was almost impossible to distinguish her from a wolf or an ice bear cub. Only the pink flesh around her eyes peeked out through the brown and gray clothing. Her eyelashes had frost on their tips. A single twist of white-blonde hair blew across her face and stuck to her half-frozen lips. When she noticed me, the edges of her eyes crinkled as though she were smiling, as if she had been waiting.

I hoisted myself over the lip of the ice, keeping my tail submerged in case she came at me with a weapon and I had to escape quickly. She rolled forward and crept toward me on her belly. I slid back into the water in alarm. I was fairly confident that her movement was not a natural human gait. It had to be a hunting creep, another way to lure prey as did her screaming. But why would she make herself so slow when there was no way she could blend in with the ice? Did humans strike like sea snakes?

The whales' heads popped up alongside me. Their blubbery bodies bobbed like little icebergs as they strained to see what had caught my interest. They chattered to each other, then caught the tension in my expression and went silent.

The human stopped her slow creep. Propping her head on her arms, she unwound the strips of fur around her mouth and cheeks. I looked into her whole face for the first time. Her skin was so pale and smooth, almost translucent, that she reminded me of one of the sculptures in our ice hall. Her features were chiseled and strong. Her jaw was sharp, almost too sharp to be beautiful, but it made her look savage and wild.

She lifted her hand and waved. That was a gesture I understood.

Hesitant, I waved back. She smiled and crawled forward until she was only a few feet from me. I ducked into the water. Behind me, two of the belugas gulped seawater and spat gallons of the freezing liquid at their former attacker. When the girl flinched, the whales grinned widely, chortling and whistling to each other. Soon the entire pod had risen to the surface, chirping and spraying freezing water that caught the sunlight and formed ice rainbows.

The human jumped to her feet and scurried away from the ice lip. "No!" she shouted, as more of the whales joined in. "No! Stop it! I'm not trying to hurt you!"

My ears perked up. The human spoke the *godstongue*.

Three

I TAPPED THE NEAREST WHALE on the nose, and he guiltily spat his water back into the sea. The others followed his lead and ducked their heads under the waves to hide from my stern glare. Sliding from the ocean, I looked at the girl. It was easy to control the belugas. They always followed orders from merfolk, and real disputes weren't in their gentle nature. But I didn't know how to read this human, who blinked rapidly and thrust out her jaw to hide her fear.

Scooting toward her on the ice, I whispered, "I understood you."

Her eyes widened as she looked me over. Then she licked her lips, which were chapped and covered with a film of sea salt, and said, "You're not supposed to exist. Everybody says the mermaids are just stories." Averting her stare, she toed a ridge on the ice. "When I saw you the other day, I thought I must have been imagining it. Hunger and swallowing salt water can make you do that."

King Calder always said that we had to protect ourselves by keeping away from prying human eyes—an easy task this far north, where few ships sailed and fewer passed through unscathed. "If they knew how to find us," the king would say, "they'd take our fish stocks, our pearls, our woven kelps… anything of value." Humans were the crabs and sharks of the land: scavengers that feasted on carrion, took more than they needed, and destroyed the homes of other species. We had to keep our home safe from them or lose everything. At least, that was what the king said.

But how was it possible the humans weren't aware of our existence at all? I beat my tail against the ice, kicking up a cloud of surface snow and showering the girl in fluffy white powder. The snowflakes caught in the tangles of her hair and glittered in the sun. "I'm real enough."

She crept forward, closing the gap between us. At this distance, I could see how the furs swathed her tiny frame. She was smaller than I'd first thought and hopelessly thin, with cheeks drawn like a wrasse fish and bones pushing at the skin around her neck. Still, she had a kind of wild beauty, with intelligent, predatory eyes like an orca or kingfisher. I reached out to touch her, as I might when meeting any other creature. Not all animals spoke the *godstongue*, but touch, I knew, could speak to all. Even the deadliest sharks of the deep calmed when we stroked them.

The human cringed and smacked my hand away. She looked at my scaled skin as if it were poisonous; her delicate nose curled. "What are you doing?"

Sensing the change in our mood, one of the belugas whistled and splashed water over the ice. He probably outweighed this fragile land creature by a hundred stone, but, like all belugas, he was unaware of his strength. I wondered how the human girl had planned to lift one of the whales from the sea all by herself, even if she had managed to spear one. Desperate hunger was not only making her believe she saw visions, but leading her to attempt the impossible as well.

A dozen more white, bald heads popped up to peer over the edge of the ice. Their cheeks bulged with water, ready to defend me in the only way they knew how. Rubbing the back of her head and relaxing now that my hand was back at my side, the girl laughed. "I'd never seen one alive before yesterday. They're ridiculous."

Though my scales glowed with fresh energy and heat from the sun, a chill passed through me. How many belugas had she seen dead? These whales were my friends. I knew the humans ate them, but the thought was enough to make me sick. Last year, this pod had lost two calves to human hunters. The raiders had scooped the babies from the sea and taken them from their families with no thought for the whales' mourning. I wondered if this girl had ever participated in hunts like those.

Her gloved hands went to a trinket at her neck, an intricately designed, heavy piece. The pendant was perfectly round, set with blue and white gemstones, and made with a shiny material I'd once been told the humans could forge only by taming the sun. With her fingers curling around it, she asked, "You must wonder why I'm here. Have you... have you ever seen a human before?"

"Before yesterday, only dead." A weight settled in my stomach, and I looked away from her. She probably thought I was the monster now. "Not that we've killed them. Shipwrecks, you know. They happen around this place a few times a year."

Even as I said it, I knew that wasn't the whole truth. Havamal had made sure I couldn't rescue the sailor who had jumped from the sinking ship. And King Calder had been quick to gather his men from the hall; he'd made sure the rest of us stayed behind and couldn't witness the humans' deaths. It was possible that the guards had made sure the sea god claimed all of them.

"We call this place the Trap, because it catches ships like a snare in the forest catches rabbits. So many people have died here, it's like a graveyard for sailors. But the whales here are so plentiful it can be worth the risk..." The girl shivered and pulled her head into her furs like a turtle retreating into its shell. When she spoke again, her voice was soft but laced with venom. "But I'm not sorry it snared *them*."

"Them?"

The human inhaled sharply. "The men who took me. The ones who owned that ship. They destroyed my entire village."

I stared at her. She was a survivor of more than one close call, it seemed. But why would the humans destroy their own settlements? I'd heard of merclans installing new rulers in settlements after a war or bringing in soldiers to restore control, but never causing destruction on that scale.

"Those sailors were privateers," she said. "Mercenaries, not whalers. Hired to loot us. I don't know what happened when they set fire to the town. They took me back to the ship, and I've been their prisoner since."

I thought of the drowning men, sinking like stones in the freezing water. I didn't know what a "privateer" was, but I understood kidnapping well enough. It was an atrocity. Learning what they had been made their deaths easier to bear.

"Why?" I asked, unsure. "What did they want with you?"

Her expression clouded and she slowly rolled up her left sleeve. I stared. The pale flesh of her arm was covered in intricate blue designs, showing the outlines of land and water. As I watched, one of the inked continents shifted, drifting like a boat across her skin. A line of red appeared. It ran from her wrist up to her forearm, where it disappeared under the fur still covering her bicep.

I reached out to touch it, to assure myself that what I was seeing was real. But she tugged her sleeve down and brought her knees up to her skinny chest.

"What is that?" I whispered. "Your tattoos… they moved."

"The navigator's marks," she said, biting her lip. "In the old days, the god Heimdallr used to visit our village. They say he fell for a girl with wild red hair and they had a child together. Ever since, every generation or two, someone is born with tattoos like these. They show you whatever you need to find."

I sucked in a deep breath. For sailors trying to navigate our treacherous waters, I could only imagine how valuable magic like that would be. The gods only bestowed their magic gifts on a few. The legendary Heimdallr, servant of Thor and god of foresight, hadn't been seen on Midgard for centuries.

"Is that why they took you?" I asked.

"They kept me in a cellar most of the time," she spat out. "Said I was a present for someone important in their home country. That's probably the only thing that stopped them from hurting me… knowing that I was a gift. Some of them were making me dance on the deck when the ship hit the iceberg. Everyone was panicking and the captain was shouting orders. They were all too busy trying to save the ship to notice me… So I gathered what supplies I could from the things on the deck, took the only lifeboat they had, and jumped."

I didn't know enough about ships to understand everything she told me. But I understood that she had condemned the men on the wooden titan to death when she took their only working craft. Death was the punishment for kidnappers under the sea, and, though I could still hear the sailors' underwater screams, I supposed they had gotten what they deserved. Aegir would see them to the afterlife.

Back shaking, she made a choked sound into her arms. "I was trained to fight. All my life. It didn't matter. They took me anyway."

This time, when I reached out to pat her shoulder, she didn't flinch. "I'm Ersel," I whispered.

She blinked back tears. Then, tugging her glove off with her teeth, she thrust out her hand. Her fingers looked as frail and brittle as dying coral. I grasped them warily and then marveled at the heat of her palm. "I'm Ragna," she said.

She pulled a little flask from her pocket and unscrewed the silver cap. The scent of fish grease drifted out. I wrinkled my nose when she pressed the bottle to her mouth and drank greedily. When she noticed my expression, Ragna shrugged. "The oil is the only food I managed to save. When it runs out, I'll starve or die of thirst, assuming I don't freeze to death first."

I covered the healthy rolls of blubber on my stomach with my arm, suddenly ashamed of how plump I must seem to her when she faced death by starvation.

Without thinking, I blurted, "I'll bring you something."

In the glacier, every family had access to our central food store. Rations were split equally from the hunts, and in recent years we hadn't struggled to find food. Since it was just the two of us, Mama and I never touched our reserves, so I knew there would be more than enough to spare. King Calder would have my scales if he caught me feeding a human, but I'd been sneaking food to the belugas for months. And the way Ragna grinned at me now—fragile and strong at the same time, like nothing I'd ever seen—was worth it. Her smile reminded me of a starfish.

Ragna pulled the ornament from her neck and thrust it at me. "Take this. I have nothing else to trade for your help."

I held the chain to the sun, studying the threads of metal. "You don't have to trade anything…"

"Look, I don't take charity," Ragna said, sniffing back the last of her tears. "Turn around. I'll fasten it on for you."

"I can't. We're not supposed to collect human things." I scooted back from her so fast I nearly dropped the necklace. Not that the rule had ever stopped me, but if I returned to the glacier wearing a human trinket like a collar around my neck, someone was bound to notice.

Her brow furrowed. "Why not?"

My eyes darted to the edge of the ice shelf. Thinking about the consequences of being caught made me feel paranoid. What if someone had followed me? Most of the glacier's inhabitants knew about the human things I collected. They insisted it was a phase I'd grow out of, like Havamal had, but if they found me talking to a real, live human? None of them would overlook that. I imagined one of the king's red-tailed guards hauling Ragna from the ice and pulling her under the sea.

"I need to get back," I said, sliding toward the water. I glided on the ice like a seal, flat on my stomach.

"Wait," she called, scrambling to her feet. "Wood. I need wood too."

I scowled. How did she expect me to get a land-growing thing to her?

When I said nothing, she reddened and rushed on. "Take it from the ship. Just pieces of the deck, or anything. I'll dry it out in the sun. My boat mostly broke when I dropped into the sea. I only just managed to make it to the shelf. I need to mend my boat to get off this ice, otherwise I might as well have drowned in the wreck."

Ripping pieces from the wooden giant wouldn't be subtle. The ship had drifted to the bottom almost directly under our fortress. If anyone saw me, I wouldn't be able to bring her food, not even a lone fish. But sunken ships littered our sea beds, some so old not even the midwife could remember a time before the floating graveyard claimed its permanent space on the ocean floor. I'd spent years scouring the hulls with Havamal for treasure. I knew nothing about wood or its durability, but if she could use materials from ships that long buried... even that presented a risk.

"Please," she insisted, touching me of her own accord. "You came back. You were curious enough to come back, so you must care at least a little. I don't want to die here."

I knew what it was like to be trapped, to feel stranded and alone.

I closed my fingers around the metal chain, hiding it in my palm. "I'll see what I can do."

WE KEPT OUR SPARE FOOD sealed behind layers of thin ice in a communal vault at the heart of the ice mountain. Two burly mermen guarded the entrance, but gaining access was easy—they couldn't stop me from taking our share. Their purpose was to keep our stores safe from wandering seals or a shark that had followed the scent of blood, not to keep the merfolk out. The guards allowed me to pass without pausing in their conversation. They didn't notice the oversized woven satchel that I carried tucked under my arm.

The inside of the vault was modeled on a coral comb, with chambers and passages dug in thick ice. A thinner layer of ice covered the opening to each cavern, protecting the food inside from creatures such as crabs that could slip through the glacier unnoticed. I swam to our comb and began beating my tail as hard as I could to fan a cyclone of water toward the fragile barrier.

The current broke the ice, and I swam inside and rested my basket on a carved-out ledge. The scents of fish, spices, and sticky, frozen blood mixed to form a perfume in the water. I hadn't eaten since breakfast. I inhaled deeply as I filled the basket to the brim with trout, shark, eel, and a bit of seaweed. Then I closed the top and fastened the attached ropes, tying the food securely inside.

I hoped that humans could eat all the things I'd packed. What if they couldn't digest shark? What if kelp made them sick? I knew that the humans occasionally hunted the white bears that roamed the ice, but I'd never heard of them eating a fish, much less an eel or a shark. There wasn't time to analyze that now that I was already a thief. I ducked my head and swept past the guards.

"Where are you going with that?" Vigdis's high-pitched voice asked behind me. "That's a lot of food. More than I pick up for my whole family when I visit them. And it's only your mother and you."

"Ellea in the cave next to us isn't well," I lied, and turned to face Vigdis. Her hands were on her full hips, and she narrowed her eyes when I spoke. "She has three small boys, so I'm picking up some things for all of them."

"Or maybe you're just planning to hide until The Grading is over." Her features smoothed in a sympathetic grimace as she looked me up and down. "It'll be okay, Ersel. You don't have to be afraid…"

"You keep acting like I'm broken," I snapped, wishing I could hurl the basket in her smug face. "You have no idea. Just leave me alone, okay?"

Vigdis flipped her hair. "You should bask today and spend more time in the sun. Your eggs are probably frozen inside you."

I didn't want to find a mate or settle into the role of mother everyone expected from me, but her assumption that I was damaged, *frozen* somewhere inside my very core, cut me. I wanted everyone to know I was making a choice, especially Vigdis. I ground my teeth. I wasn't afraid. I knew my body was strong. "What time is The Grading? When does the mage arrive?"

I should have known, but I'd been trying my hardest to block it out.

"Sundown."

If I swam quickly, I might be back in time to prove them all wrong—or right, an insidious little voice inside me argued. The king wouldn't make me find a mate *immediately*. I could plan my escape. I'd been ruminating on it long enough.

Ragna would have to wait for the wood to fix her raft. It was noon already and winter, when days were short. My stomach fluttered. I had so many questions for the human girl, and I'd waited a lifetime to ask. I wanted to bring her each of my treasures in turn, and go through them one by one. But as soon as she fixed her boat, she'd sail away, and I needed to leave as well.

Pushing Vigdis aside, I sped down the hall before my tears could warm the water around her. I couldn't let her know that she'd hurt me.

By the time I reached the ice shelf, my breath came in gasps. I even struggled to push myself from the water and onto the ice as exhaustion clawed at me. Who was I kidding? As tired as I was, there was no way my grading would go well.

Ragna waited beside the ice hole with her legs curled under her. She was scratching the tongue of one of the bolder belugas. The whale flapped his fins jubilantly, bobbed his head, and opened his jaw wider so she could reach the back of his mouth. Ragna was laughing. Her thin frame shook so hard she nearly slipped into the ocean.

She didn't notice me at first, but when I flexed my aching tail and groaned in relief, she looked up. Catching sight of the bursting satchel, her eyes grew bright as a sea eel's. "Is all that for me?"

"Will it be enough?" I knew nothing about how humans fed. How fast did they digest? They were in the sun all the time, continuously charging their skins. All of that sunlight had to give them energy. But then why was Ragna was so bony?

"This will keep me for a month," she said, chuckling. "And it's easy to keep it frozen, but I'll have to use some of my fish oil to cook it. Did you bring the wood?"

"Cook it?" I knew the *godstongue*, but words or concepts related to fire, I never quite understood. We couldn't make fire in the ocean. Did she mean to burn the fish? A bolt of dread went through me. Maybe she wasn't going to eat it. Some of the gods liked their sacrifices eviscerated by smoke, Heimdallr included. She couldn't mean to offer all the food I'd smuggled.

"You know, heat it up? Make it not raw? So you can eat it?"

My nose wrinkled in disgust. She wanted to eat quality food hot. Everyone knew that food rotted it when it got warm. I'd never experienced a summer, but Mama said that when she was a child and our pod sometimes ventured south to the summer waters, she had seen fish bloated with worms and dead whales whose carcasses filled with gas until they exploded. Ragna wanted to eat that! The idea was so disgusting I almost vomited into the ocean.

She chuckled, then winked at me. "I forget you live your whole life underwater. The whole cooking thing probably doesn't make a lot of sense to you. It's good, though, trust me."

I stuck out my tongue and made a gagging noise at the back of my throat.

Ragna took another long drink from her flask of fish oil.

The low winter light dimmed further as a cloud covered the sun. I squinted at the sky. It would be sundown in less than an hour. I needed to leave quickly if I was to prove myself at the ceremony. "I have to go. I'll bring the wood you need tomorrow and some things I want to ask you about—some human items."

Mischievousness sparkled in her dark eyes. "Items? I thought you weren't supposed to keep things that belong to us?"

I chewed my lip. "We're not… but I've collected a few. I just want to know how they work, what they do…"

"So you keep all those things but you were wary of my necklace? I think you just didn't like it." She pressed her lips together. "Are you saying my pendant is ugly?"

"No!" I snapped, irritated at how she was turning the conversation around. "I just can't have something so obvious. I kept your necklace. I'm just not wearing it."

Ragna giggled; her fake frown disappeared. "Are all mermaids this easy to wind up?"

I glared at her.

"We'll trade again. My knowledge for wood."

I sighed, then rolled my eyes. With the stress of The Grading, I couldn't recognize a little gentle teasing. "It's a deal."

Gathering up the basket of food in her skinny arms, Ragna stumbled to her feet. "I'm starting to feel faint. I'm going to go cook this."

That was my cue to leave. Nothing sounded less appealing to me than watching how she destroyed our food. Besides, I knew I had to hurry. I scooted to the edge of the glacier. Ragna gave me a one-handed salute, then shuffled into her makeshift shelter. I'd see her tomorrow, after she'd desecrated the fish.

Tomorrow, I thought, watching her pull the curtain of fur closed behind her, *when The Grading was over and everything could be different.*

Four

MAMA'S FINGERS TWISTED THROUGH MY hair, threading oyster pearls and tiny shells into my long blue locks. The pearls had been my idea—a little extra decoration to illuminate the topaz lights in my thick hair. Vigdis thought I never saw the sun because I never drew attention to the subtle lights in my hair or the freckles across my nose. I wanted to show her up in more ways than one. Mama took a green net of the finest weave I'd ever seen and fashioned it into a short veil over my eyes.

Her fingers quivered as she braided the net into place. "You don't have to do this, you know." Her voice shook as badly as her hands. "I've always imagined, well, that you might do something else. You always talked about it when you were a child. Maybe you could ask Aegir's mage to take you back to the sea god's court. It's happened before."

"No one acts like there's a choice," I said with an agitated sigh. "And if I go with the mage, I'd just be another kind of prisoner."

Mama stroked my head. "I know there's a lot of pressure. We could try to delay it. We might buy you some time—"

One of the pearls slipped down into my lap. Looking up, I saw that Mama was crying. "Do you ever wish you just started weaving right away? That you hadn't hatched me?"

"Oh, gods, no." She spun me around to face her. Wrinkles of concern lined her forehead and creased her eyes. "But I'd be lying if I told you I wasn't sometimes glad your father died young. There was never any love between us. I let him choose me because I thought I had to accept whoever asked for me. If he hadn't passed, maybe I'd still be brooding eggs. I imagine that sometimes and it gives me nightmares. It's not easy. Don't make a decision just to prove something to your friends."

My hand found hers and covered it. "Mama, I'm just going so they'll stop talking. For all we know, I might be infertile. And if someone asks me, I don't have to say yes."

Her arms wrapped around me, and she pulled me close. The water around her was warm with emotion. "You might get swept up. It's easy to do. A young merman approaches you, and before you know it, you've agreed, even if you didn't mean to, even if you didn't *want* him…"

We broke apart. I shook my head until all the pearls fell out. They floated around us, suspended in the water like stars. If I was going just to prove myself, then there was no need for me to dress up. The mage from the god's court only cared about what was inside my womb, not what jewelry I wore. Mama snatched the pearls from the sea and stuffed them back inside the little clamshell pouch she wore at her hip.

"I'm not like that, Mama. None of them interest me."

"Not even Havamal?" She winked at me, but her eyes were tired. "He's gotten awfully good-looking."

"No, especially not him. And don't remind me. Everyone's always fawning over him." A lump rose in my throat. Havamal was mated to a world—a system—where I didn't belong. He couldn't have both that world and me.

"Someday, I hope you two work it out." She pressed a kiss against my cheek. "Not that I want you rushing into a mating bond, but you used to be such close friends."

I choked back a sob and closed my eyes to hide the tears brewing under my lids. "I'll leave now. If I get there early, maybe I can speak to the mage alone."

"Whatever she tells you, remember you make your own decisions. And your egg count is not what makes you."

"Tell that to Vigdis," I muttered. After giving her a final hug, I swam out of Mama's crevice and into my own. My eyes swept the chamber, looking for something I could carry. I wanted something small to remind me of the things I valued, something I could hold on to if I were tempted to betray myself.

Pushing aside the kelp curtain, I fished around in my carved bin for Ragna's necklace. She'd survived capture, imprisonment, and a shipwreck on her own. This ornament had dangled from her neck through all of it. I bit my lip, then fastened the chain around my neck. The delicate metal was numbingly cold against my scales, but the sheer defiance of wearing the necklace inside the glacier thrilled me. If he saw it, King Calder would be beyond furious, but I was already bending to pressure by attending the ceremony. My hair was long and thick. If I had to, I could hide the necklace with my hair.

With my chin held high, I swam to the great hall and passed through the arches. I was early, so the hall was nearly empty, but the king sat on his dais, flanked by a troop of guards. On his right, the sea god's court mage sat on a low stool helping herself to cuts of fish from a tray in Havamal's hands. The king whispered into her ear. He ignored Havamal's presence completely. The mage cackled into her spindly hands. I wondered how Havamal felt, being treated like an invisible part of the landscape, a beautiful serving plate, when he had signed on as a warrior.

The mage had the legged body of a human. Most of her was doughy and pink, but her skin was pocked with barnacles that had attached directly to her flesh. Algae-covered gills gaped at her neck, and she wheezed when she tried to suck in water. I'd always considered myself lucky to have a mermaid's gills: dozens of tiny flaps concealed under our scales. Looking at the woundlike structures on her neck made me more intensely grateful. Long, twisted strands of seaweed seemed to grow from her head where hair should have been; the locks sprouted in mismatched shades of green, deep coral, and topaz.

She was the strangest looking creature I'd ever seen.

Havamal rested the tray on the nearest table and backed up to the wall. His eyes widened when he saw me, but then narrowed when the glimmering necklace at my throat drew his attention. He missed nothing. I combed my long hair around my neck to cover it. Now that I was in the king's presence, my nerve failed me.

"Ersel," King Calder said in his hoarse cough of a voice. "I didn't expect you to be the first. I was led to believe you weren't excited about the ceremony."

Had Havamal told him that? Or had some other insidious little fish, Vigdis perhaps, been whispering in his ear?

Hastily, I sank into a bow, dipping my chin lower than etiquette demanded to be sure the necklace was fully hidden. The intensity in the king's eyes made the hairs on the back of my neck prickle. I felt subversive with his stare on me, as though I wore a dangerous secret instead of a simple chain.

"I'm ready for it to be finished," I admitted, lightening my words with a falsely confident smile. I didn't know where he got his information about me, but all of us knew about the king's vicious changes in mood. He had never seemed to take any interest in me before, so now that he remembered anything about me, I was nervous. Although he seemed happy enough in this moment, I knew what happened to those who lied to him. Liars earned his most capricious responses—above the disobedient, the unruly, and the drunk.

When I was eleven, right after the king took power from his mother, his sister had lied to him about her whereabouts. After summoning the bailiff, the king ordered his guards to hold her fast while the enforcer removed one of her rear scales with a pair of tongs. I heard the girl's screams in my nightmares for a week.

She had been the rightful heir to the throne; the king was only ruling as regent until she came of age. Girl children had the first right of inheritance. That had always been our law before King Calder seized power. The princess had been a frail child and constantly ill. Calder had bullied her into letting him reign as regent and controlled her with cruelty. When the princess died, some people had thought her lucky.

Aegir's mage laid her gnarled hand on the king's shoulder. "The first girl is here; you must take your leave."

He stiffened at her touch. "I'm the king in this glacier. I should be privy to what goes on here. My mother always stayed."

"Your mother did always oversee the proceedings. Yes, boy, I know." The mage's eyes crinkled, and she laughed. "But your mother was a woman. No merman has ever seen these rites, and you will not be the first. You may be a king in this ice mountain, but I am a member of the sea god's court and I outrank you in every possible way. I remind you of this yearly. A girl is here, and we will begin."

"My mother pushed me out of the proceedings too, and it was a mistake that cost us," Calder growled. "She put too much faith in Inkeri."

The mage's lips parted, revealing rows of green-stained teeth. "Your mother wasn't the one at fault concerning your sister."

"It's getting more important," he hissed as his fingers tightened on the arms of this throne. "Our future—"

"I know what importance this has to you." The old woman's glare was hard as fresh ice. "But I serve Aegir, not you. And if anything happens to me, you will answer to him. The sea god does not forget, nor does he forgive. Begone."

I held my breath as the king's blue-scaled fingers balled into fists. Surely he wouldn't hurt a messenger of the gods, even one who had threatened him? The captain of the King's Guard cleared his throat and gestured toward the hall's archway. "Your Majesty, I hear the gatherers have the feast prepared. It's laid out in the small hall." The merman chanced a wink at his king. "If we wait there, we can appraise each girl when she comes out. Perhaps help young Havamal choose a mate."

A few of the other guards tittered. A handful looked ashamed and wouldn't meet my eye. One pinched Havamal's cheek.

I wanted to scream.

The king rested his hand on his belly and paused to look the shadow mage up and down in an obvious challenge. The old woman crossed her arms over her bony chest. Then he burst into a roar of laughter and clapped Havamal hard on the back. Speaking to the captain, he said, "You're right, Heiden. It's high time this one found the girl he's been searching for. He's certainly good-looking enough."

Havamal stole a glance at me. The hope in his eyes burned even brighter than his cheeks. It scalded my heart. Hastily, I turned away and studied the ice table. A shallow crack ran the length of its surface, and I traced it with a finger in a vain attempt to seem as if I weren't paying any attention to him. If he believed I'd give up everything—my freedom—to choose him, he couldn't know me at all. But that hope in his eyes... everything in me ached.

The king and his procession filed from the hall, most of the men joking with Havamal. I could feel his eyes on me as he swam away, but I refused to look at him. Even after his betrayal, I didn't relish causing him pain.

As soon as the mermen had gone, Aegir's mage stumbled toward me on her strange land-legs. She settled herself on a stool and took my hand in hers. Warmth flooded through my scales, as if she held the sun between her fingers. "You're not here to find a mate."

"Of course I am..." I stammered, but she pressed her finger to my lips.

"I can always tell the girls who are just here to prove something. But wanting what you want isn't anything to be ashamed of, and what you desire is none of my business. I'm not here to pass judgment, only to give information." She squeezed my hand comfortingly.

"But our future is determined by that information! We're judged on it for the rest of our lives!" I exclaimed. How could the mage believe she wasn't responsible for passing judgment? Mermaids in the glacier lived with the result of her pronouncements every day. We could take The Grading next year, should we fail, but the stigma of a low follicle count clung to us like a scale infection, lingering for a lifetime. Worse still, none of us knew what to expect from the ceremony itself.

"I give this information at the request of your king and community. Members of my order have always assisted when it comes to matters of the womb—for all the creatures who dwell in Aegir's realm." She sighed, cupping my chin with her free hand. "But it's not me who decides to give your fertility so much value."

I pulled away from her as hot tears threatened to spill down my cheeks. Biting my lip, I managed to hold them in check. I didn't want anyone to come in, feel the warm water around me, and think I was a coward. I'd come here to prove myself, but now I felt even more powerless in the face of our merclan's expectations.

Some part of me had always wished I could blame the gods for the way we did things and our laws. Our kingdom had struggled to hatch live children ever since the clans migrated to the harsher winter world from the southern world. We'd lost a war, and the price of our defeat had been exile. Life in the ice chilled our wombs and made eggs difficult to incubate after they were laid.

In my clutch, Mama had laid a dozen eggs, and I was the only one to hatch.

A group of mermaids swam into the hall. Their giggles echoed down the hallway after them. It shouldn't have bothered me, but I felt a pang of jealousy seeing them all arrive together, so obviously friends. Vigdis swam at the head of their little column like a general leading her troops into battle. Most of the other girls had dressed for the occasion. Their long hair contained mother-of-pearl fragments, rare shells, and finely woven nets. Many wore iridescent cloaks of stretched jellyfish skin that blinked blue, then pink, in the pale light of the glacier's interior. Seeing them like that, together and in all their finery, I felt small and even more exposed.

When Vigdis saw me sitting with the mage, her eyebrows rose almost to her hairline. She rushed to sit on the mage's other side, exclaiming, "Ersel! I didn't expect to see you here… early?" Then she schooled her voice into that patronizing sympathy. "Wanted to get it over with before the rest of us arrived? I understand."

I clenched my jaw and glared at her.

Aegir's mage was unfazed. She patted Vigdis on the hand. "There, there, dear. You'll get your chance too. Ersel has simply volunteered to go first." She turned to me with a twinkle in her eyes. My heart leapt into my mouth. First? No… "I have a feeling she's going to get excellent results."

One of Vigdis's cohort, Rayne, snorted. "Not likely. She practically hides from the sun."

I wanted to punch Rayne in her smug face, but the mage's stated confidence comforted me and made the situation a little easier to tolerate.

"What is your birth season, child?" The mage asked, brushing my hair back off my shoulders. I heard the collective gasp as the human pendant was exposed. But as before, her fingers left a trail of warmth and quieted my fear.

"*Haustr*," I replied. I was a child of the deep autumn; a child of death and grayness and so, maybe, as cold to the core as everyone imagined.

The mage's smile widened, revealing rows of sharpened teeth that overlapped like a shark's. "Uncommon in a mermaid, to be sure. But *haustr* is Loki's season, so she may surprise us all. The trickster is known to have a game or two up their sleeve."

I never thought of myself as a child of Loki. *Haustr* was Baldr's season as well, and I preferred to think of myself as a child of the god of love and joy rather than of deception. Still, it couldn't hurt to murmur an extra prayer to Loki now. I cast my eyes toward their bust on the ceiling and silently mouthed the words to one of the incantations I'd known since childhood. Staring up at the imposing ice statue, I could have sworn Loki's glassy lips curled into a smile.

"Ready?" the mage asked. I looked back at her and jumped in shock. Her appearance had totally changed. She was glowing brighter than any jellyfish cloak. Pure sunlight seemed to emanate from her very pores; the wrinkles that had lined her eyes had smoothed away. The barnacles were gone, replaced by the smoothest beluga-white flesh. The other girls in the hall gasped. She smiled. "Climb up onto the table and lie back. Let's see what we're working with."

I did as she instructed while the other girls gathered round. With their eyes on me, I felt like a prized catch, about to be butchered and divided up for a grand dinner or the Nacht feast. Considering how many mermen would be waiting with the king for the results, ready to catch a prize of their own, maybe I was right to feel that way. If my grading went well, they'd all see me as something to hunt.

Havamal doesn't see you that way, a voice in my head insisted before I silenced it. Maybe once that had been true. Now I didn't know what he saw when he looked at me.

The mage stretched her fingers over my belly. Then she began to massage the fleshy area above the line of my tail scales. Her deft hands kneaded my doughy stomach and I allowed myself a small grin of satisfaction. Vigdis could say what she liked about my sunbathing habits, but I ate well, and my body showed it. Even if the mage could only find a single follicle, my fat reserves could nourish a hundred developing eggs. I cringed inwardly. I didn't *want* children, so why was I proud of that?

A sudden blast of heat cut through me. I struggled for breath as pain coursed in waves through my stomach and down into my tail. My back arched, and I let out a strangled cry. I'd never experienced pain like this. It was dizzying in its intensity, clawing at my insides. The heat abated, but it was replaced by a pulling sensation, almost like a rope tightening around my organs, dragging them out through my mouth. I screamed and screamed, trying desperately to grip the slippery ice table and steady my struggling body.

No wonder our mothers were forbidden to tell us about the ceremony. If I had known about the pain I would experience, I might have decided to hell with Vigdis. Her opinion of me wasn't worth this torture. Above me, the mage was chanting. Her eyes glowed white, and she didn't seem to see me. I thrashed on the ice table, and my tears made the room warm.

Then a sensation like liquid ice moved up my throat, forcing my mouth open. I tried to swallow, but a mist of glowing orbs erupted from inside me. They scattered in the water around us like multicolored stars: some turquoise blue, others green or coral, a few the same piercing silver as Havamal's fins. The pain vanished almost as quickly as it had begun. I sat up and stared in awe at the orbs.

The old mage's eyes regained their sharpness. She smiled at me and stroked my cheek with a long finger. Standing, she twirled with her arms spread wide. The orbs followed her fingers as if pulled by a current, forming a glittering cyclone around her.

A collective gasp rose in the hall.

"Are those... eggs?" Vigdis asked, looking at me. The pity in her eyes was gone, replaced by pure hatred.

"No," the mage laughed. She snatched one of the delicate silver balls from the air and held it to her cheek. The little ball took on her glow and began to hum softly, almost like a lullaby. "They're voices. All the voices she has the potential to create."

After releasing the orb and letting it float away, the old woman squeezed my bicep. "The best result I've seen in decades. It would be fruitless to count. You could hatch as many children as you desire." The wrinkles slowly etched themselves back around the corners of her eyes and mouth as she spoke. "But I know that isn't what you desire. You're a *haustr* child through and through. Full of paradoxes. Loki is playing their little jokes with you."

Feeling suddenly drained and heavy, I wrapped my arms around my chest. Everyone was staring at me. Everyone was *jealous* of me. I should feel overjoyed. I'd showed them. Vigdis would never again be able to say there was something wrong with me.

But there was, wasn't there? I wasn't like the other mermaids. And the little silver orbs that shimmered so much like Havamal's scales as they hummed their sweet ballads just made me feel all the more broken.

Five

I DIDN'T WAIT AS THE others queued up to face the mage's touch. The walls of the fortress bore down on me, and I needed to get into the open sea. The orbs' voices followed me as I rushed for the hall's exit. They seeped straight into my skin as I swam, as if my body were made of nothing but water.

The mage called out to me, and a few of the other girls tried to grab my arms, but I pushed past them. I didn't need to hear any congratulations they were going to offer. And I definitely didn't want to know whatever the mage would say next.

A row of curious mermen waited by the hall's exit. No doubt they were trying to get a first glimpse of the girls before the rest of the suitors, who waited with the king. I swallowed a lump of bile. The mermen moved aside when I swam past. The oldest, a blue-finned sentry, gave me a look that was almost pitying. They thought I had failed and couldn't face it.

The irony made me want to laugh and scream at the same time. Aegir's mage showed us the voices we had the potential to create, while our king stripped us of our own voices and condemned us to years brooding in chambers like prisons. No one ever asked me what I wanted. Our glacier's need to survive had turned us all into slaves of this ritual and the king's ugly pride.

I knew that the ceremony would last through the day and into the night. A feast would follow once all the mermaids had their results. If I left now, I could disappear until sundown before anyone would miss me. It might be the only opportunity I'd get to bring wood for Ragna.

I wasn't willing to risk raiding Ragna's own ship for materials. It was too close to the glacier. Any number of feasters, drunk on soured dolphin milk, could wander off looking for a quiet place to rest, or a place to mate if they were some of the newly paired. I shuddered. I couldn't think about the aftermath of the ritual.

Would Havamal choose someone else? The question sent a wave of nausea through me. As a member of the King's Guard, there would be more pressure on him to find a match. I imagined him with his Vigdis as his strong arms curled around her coral tail. Rage shot through me like a lightning bolt. I didn't want the life he'd chosen, but the thought of him with someone else hurt almost as badly as the mage's inspection.

I swam for the wreck I knew best, located a mile or so beyond the beluga's surfacing hole. It was an ancient ship, half buried in the sand, rusted and rotting despite the cold of the water. A school of silver-finned herring came out to greet me as I dove into the ship's hollow interior. The skeletons of a hundred dead humans leaned against the walls. Stray bones—fingers, ribs, and toes—were scattered over the decaying deck.

I trembled. The sight of the eyeless skulls and scattered bones had never bothered me before. As a child, Havamal sometimes picked up the skull fragments and wore them as masks. I would giggle as he rammed his head into the walls to impress me with his makeshift armor. But that was before I'd met a human: before I'd seen the depth, intelligence, even empathy, in Ragna's eyes; before I knew that humans spoke the *godstongue* and smiled like starfish.

I swallowed another sob. What did it say about my life that, when everything was falling apart, the only being I could go to for comfort was a human I barely knew? An enemy.

I wrapped my fingers around her pendant and held it tightly. Ragna was the only one who understood what it meant to feel like a prisoner. Right now, I needed whatever level of understanding we had.

The least decayed part of the ship was at its very center. Shielded from the elements and the less adventurous scavenger crabs, most of the interior remained sodden but intact. A lone skeleton lay on the remains of a framed box in the enclosed cabin. I supposed humans used the boxes as beds, though they didn't look very comfortable. He held a pair of rusting crossed blades over his bare ribs. Swallowing distaste, I pried one of the blades from his brittle fingers. I swished it through the water, hoping it would be strong enough to help me break pieces of the fragile wood from the ship's walls.

Behind me, someone cleared his throat. I whirled around, raising the blade.

"I thought I might find you here," Havamal said. He swam slowly toward me, hand half raised, as if to calm me as he would a frightened whale. "I asked about you when the first girl came through. I was worried about how nervous you'd be. And how safe, especially after I saw that human pendant you were wearing. She said you'd gone first. The sentry said he'd seen you swim off."

So he was tracking me now, inquiring after my every movement. Annoyance bubbled up inside me. This was supposed to be my chance. "So you thought you'd just chase after me? Did it even occur to you that I might want to be alone?"

"The next girl to come out said that you passed... that you were the best in decades." A small smile lit up his face. He swam closer and rested his hand on my back. "That's great. I'm so proud of you. You don't have to be afraid of it anymore."

Proud of me? He was *proud* of me? With all my strength, I pushed him away and into the wall behind him. "I was *never* afraid. I did it because I was tired of Vigdis saying there was something wrong with me."

Wincing from the impact, Havamal muttered, "Well, you won't have to worry about Vigdis saying anything ever again."

"That's right!" I snapped.

Havamal took a seat on the edge of a wooden chest and crossed his muscular arms over his chest. His beautiful, pure silver scales twinkled in the dim light and reflected in his eyes. He whispered in a conspiratorial tone, "She's not fertile. Only two eggs."

Even though I knew what kind of person it made me, my heart soared. All those years of enduring Vigdis's teasing and veiled insults, and, it turned out, she was the one who was broken!

It was too easy to slip back into the easy mode we'd always shared, gossiping together in the hull of the dead ship. With news like that, I couldn't stay angry at him. "What?" I sat beside him and rested the blade over my lap. "Two? Are you serious?"

He nodded emphatically. "Just two. She's beside herself."

I covered my mouth, stifling a giggle. I knew I shouldn't laugh, but I couldn't help it.

Plucking the sword from my lap, Havamal examined the edge of the blade. Then his deft fingers traced the clouded jewels on the hilt. "I can't believe you stole from a corpse, even if it's a human. Thor's going to zap you all the way from Asgard, you know."

I punched his arm. "Like we haven't done it before a thousand times. Thor doesn't care what the merfolk do."

He snorted, returning the blade to my lap. "Me, never. You've always been the rebel."

"You sure? I seem to remember that you were the one convincing me to sneak out at night."

He rubbed the back of his head. "I'm not confirming."

A moan pealed through the ship as a strong wave passed overhead. Havamal's fingers brushed the blue scale patterns on my palm. I let my weight sag into the reassuring and familiar firmness of his torso. A deep breath escaped, and a feeling like relief made my body feel boneless. How long had it been since we had done this?

"Erie," he whispered, bringing his fingers up to toy with a curl in my hair. Hesitantly, he touched the ornament around my neck and rubbed the detailed engravings with his thumb. Bubbles from his breath tickled my earlobe. "I still love you, you know."

A sob caught inside me. Whatever easiness I'd felt vanished. He always had to ruin things. "Did you come here to convince me… convince me to be your mate?"

He shook his head. "Nah. I know you'll need some time."

I looked up into his storm-gray eyes and his full, blood-red lips. I had to be honest with him, even though it hurt both of us. "I don't know if time is what I need."

Havamal stiffened, and when he spoke again, his voice sounded forced. "I know you want to explore. I know you want your freedom… whatever that means. And I'm sorry that isn't what I want anymore. I'm happy here. I have a position. I want to build a life."

I nodded, setting my jaw. "We had plans to build a life."

"We had stupid childish dreams," he snapped, throwing up his hands. "You really think we could make it out there? Just the two of us? Swimming endlessly around the ocean forever?"

"We could have made it to the south," I said. "Everyone knows our kind haven't lived in this ice cave forever."

"And what, you'd leave all our friends? Your Mama?"

"I don't have any friends! All anyone ever talks about is the ceremony and about finding mates." I tried to ignore what he said about Mama. She'd be all alone and the thought of that made something die inside me. But she would understand, and I knew she'd be happy for me. She knew why I couldn't stay. She'd be relieved that I'd gone somewhere better.

"Well, I do!" He yelled back, squaring his shoulders. "And I don't want to feel torn between them and you."

"Then choose them!" I screamed. "I'm not asking you to choose me, because I won't choose you if it means I have to stay here. You're not worth that to me."

My whole body trembled with anger and pain, but I was way past the point of tears. We'd always argued, even when we were kids. But now there was venom in the water between us. We poisoned each other whenever we were together.

"I don't want to spend my life alone in the dark," I whispered.

"You think I would do that to you?" He sighed and closed his eyes, and I watched his expression change as he forced his anger down deep. Then his fingers cupped my chin, gentle but shaking. "It would be your choice. Always your choice. But I didn't come here to fight. Just promise me there's no one else?"

A choked laugh erupted from me and I shoved him, but there was no vehemence in it. "Of course there's no one else. I can't even tolerate anyone else."

That teased a smile from him. Brushing my hair behind my ears, he got up and hovered in the water in front of me. "Just promise me you'll think about it?"

I sighed and didn't protest any further, because arguing with him only hurt both of us. "I will."

He nodded and tried to wink. "I'll leave you to your grave-robbing." Then he swam away, fast as a harpoon, head tucked against his chest.

I clutched the rusting sword so tightly it cut into my palm. Blood blossomed into the sea, unfurling like a sea anemone. A warm current streamed behind Havamal toward me. I leaned my head back against the ship's decaying walls and broke as his tears bathed me in heat.

THE HUMAN SWORD MADE A poor tool, and I ended up stripping wood from the ship's hull with my fingers, prying the metal bolts out one by one. The ship's age made the wood soft, but by the time I had a small stack of wood and nails, my hands were bleeding and my muscles screamed.

A curious white shark poked his nose into the chamber, drawn by the scent of my blood. Sharks didn't harm mermaids on purpose, and with gentle coaxing I managed to get the beast to ram the ship's hull. The force of his impact sent shards of wood flying. I scooped them up in tired arms, praying that the wood I gathered would be enough to mend Ragna's boat.

I swam along the sea bottom so no one would see me. Sparse weeds and strands of kelp brushed against my scales, making me itch. Once I was under the belugas' breathing hole, I could deposit the heavy materials and call on the whales for assistance in bringing things to the surface. I knew that, as heavy as the wood seemed underwater, I would never manage to heave it over the lip of the ice.

A ring of light appeared on the dark seafloor. I looked up, watching the twisting bodies of the whales. They looked slimmer by the day. Schools of fish were becoming scarcer, as the humans got bolder and expanded their hunting grounds ever closer to the ice. And the merclan was harvesting most of the crabs and octopi from the sands. I would have to show the matriarch the silverfin that were making their home in the ship's decaying husk. Those tuna could feed the whale pod for weeks.

After depositing the wood in the sand, I swam to the light. The matriarch greeted me, and I gestured at the wood. She nudged my arm with her great head and trilled to a group of loitering, chattering juveniles. One of the juveniles blew a cheeky ring of bubbles in her direction, but the group scattered nonetheless, swimming down to retrieve my materials. I stroked the matriarch's snout, grateful as always for these gentle sea ghosts who helped without question.

A giant tail thrashed in the water above. My gaze jerked up. The whale's body was outside the water, but his massive tail swirled in the sea. My heart skipped a beat. Was it possible that Ragna had lured one of the creatures to its death? Had that been her plan in watching me? To learn how to soothe the creatures well enough that her meals would come to her?

I sped for the surface, then breached with all my strength. I used the momentum from my kick to propel me into the air and up over the ice's lip. With a painful thud, I landed on the ice and then looked for the stranded whale. A trio of belugas were lined up on the ice in front of Ragna. Their great tails beat in the water with excitement. A few of the fish I'd brought her lay in a gruesome pile at her feet, chopped into bloody pieces.

"First you!" Ragna directed, pointing to a creamy white male. She glanced at me and smiled. Her cheeks looked rosier and fuller. The beluga opened his mouth and emitted a guttural hum. She turned her attention to a speckled female. The whale's eyes followed her fingers, and she counted a silent beat and then pointed. The speckled female's higher voice rose to join the male's. The sound they made together was beautiful—ethereal and resonant, echoing around the silence of the ice. Ragna tossed a piece of fish into each whale's gaping mouth.

Pivoting to look at the last whale, a tiny male with scars from a polar bear's brutal claws etched over his back, Ragna sighed. His black eyes danced as they followed her, but when she pointed to him, he made a screeching noise so awful I had to cover my ears.

Ragna grimaced but then flashed the whale a grin. She tossed fish into his mouth and knelt to pat his back.

Guilt flooded through me. Of course she hadn't been trying to lure them to their deaths. I'd already learned she wasn't a monster. From the look of things, I'd brought her more than enough provisions. It warmed my heart that she was sharing with the creatures I loved.

"He can't sing at all, bless him," she chuckled as she tickled the whale's chin.

I shuffled over to sit beside her. Warmth hovered in the air around her, and the soft fur on her coat brushed against my side. My skin prickled where we touched, and I became acutely aware of the molding of my body against hers. Her smile was infectious. As I listened to the whales sing, some of the stress of The Grading and my encounter with Havamal started to melt away. It was peaceful here with her, sitting on the surface, and totally removed from the world I hated below.

The juvenile whales began to push the wood I'd gathered over the ledge onto the ice. Ragna's smile grew wider. "You managed." She jumped to her feet and half slid on the ice to the pile. Her gloved hands felt along each piece of wood. "They're old, but some drying in the sun should make them sturdy enough to patch the holes in the boat. Thank you."

"Where will you go?" I asked. "You said your home was destroyed. Will there be anything left for you to go back to?"

Ragna glanced up at me, and the gleam in her brown eyes darkened. "Oh, I'm not going back there. Not yet." Her teeth flashed, bright white against her wind-chapped lips. Were all human teeth so sharp? "I was supposed to be a gift for someone. I wouldn't want to disappoint him by failing to arrive." She looked out across the sea and played with the edge of her furs. "I'm a long way from home… and when I last saw it, everything was ash. We've been sailing for weeks, but the sailors were getting excited. They were almost back to their own homes."

She pushed back her sleeve and stared at the moving tattoos on her arm. They shifted, arranging into a jagged landmass with bays and names sketched in miniscule script. I moved closer, squinting at the names of places I couldn't imagine. What did a city look like on land? I imagined the chaos and noise of the ships magnified a hundredfold—all those people.

I traced the coastline that extended onto her palm. The tattoos were so strange and, as with so many things about her, I should have been afraid, but I wasn't. There was something eerily beautiful about these god's marks. "Does it hurt you? When these change?"

Ragna shrugged. "I feel it. It's like a prickle, but I'm used to it. And it's worth it… to always know the way to things you desire."

Something about the way she said that word… *desire…* made me blush and look down at my lap. "Why would you want to go there? They captured you. Aren't you worried they could take you prisoner again?"

"Where else am I going to go?" She looked toward the far horizon. "I'm pretty sure my family are dead. My home is ruined. I want answers. I want to know why they attacked us so brutally. They won't realize I survived, so it'll be easy for me to sneak up on them."

I understood her reaction. I wanted answers, too, whenever Mama hinted at our clan's past. Once we had lived in caves carved into the coral reefs, in water warm enough to heat our scales so we never had to surface. I never understood why we left, or why the royalty had banned us from talking about it.

But that had happened many generations ago, before anyone alive could remember, so I had no witnesses to question. And it wasn't as if I had the pain of fresh memory, like Ragna did now. Havamal and I used to talk about visiting the clans that were still living in the south, seeking our fortunes there. A ball of pain burst inside me. I pressed my hand to my throat, nodding to Ragna without words. I wasn't going to think about Havamal.

"Are you all right?" she asked. Her acute brown eyes scanned my face and then moved to my throat. "You're wearing it." A huge smile bloomed across her face; the clouds of vengeance cleared from her expression.

I returned her grin. "We had a ceremony today. I didn't really want to go, so I wore this as... a rebellion, I guess."

Ragna curled her legs under her, sitting in a jumbled position. I wondered what it would be like to have such flexibility, to be able to move my body and legs into so many arrangements. "What kind of ceremony? Where do you live? How do you live? I know nothing about anything of yours."

I smiled, thinking of the human trinkets I'd stowed away. I was equally curious about them, and wanted to ask her what the items were for. "It's a grading. They try to find out how fertile we are," I said, picking at a rough scale on my fin. "Then all the mermen sort of swarm us, trying to decide who they should pick as a mate."

"You don't get to choose?"

"We can say no, I guess... but mostly we don't. There's a lot of pressure, and I don't know what our king would do. We can't...

we don't… it's not easy for us to have children here." I ground my teeth in frustration. "If you're fertile, the clan says it's your duty."

"It sounds awful." Ragna moved so close to me that I could feel the warmth of her breath against my back. It was nice, though it made my scales stand on end, stretching toward the heat. Then she squeezed my shoulders in a gruff, one-armed hug. "It was the same for me, back home, but when I was younger. My adoptive father was always talking about making arrangements for me. He used to say it would keep me safe. But then I learned to fight, and they forgot all that."

The hunter's smile was back. She wasn't monstrous, as we had been led to believe humans were, but there was something dangerous about her nonetheless. Courage that ran so deep I could almost feel it coursed through her. What would it have been like, to survive on a ship alone? To be taken from your home as a gift to a foreign leader? To jump from the deck of a sinking titan, with no certainty that you'd survive?

If I were half as brave as she was, I would dive into the ocean right now and swim away without another thought. I'd make my own destiny.

"I want to fight, but I don't know how," I whispered. My stomach clenched with ghost pain from the mage's hands.

The nearest whale pushed his nose into Ragna's hand. She looked thoughtful as she reached inside his opened mouth to scratch the back of his tongue. "Sometimes you won't have a plan," she said fiercely. "Sometimes you'll jump before you have time to think, and it'll work out okay. I can't afford to be afraid anymore, even though I feel fear pulling at me. I'm never going to be a prisoner again. Not anyone's. Not even inside my own mind."

I CREPT BACK TO THE glacier late that evening, after the sun had disappeared behind the gray mountains at the edge of the ice shelf. I'd spent the rest of the evening watching Ragna as she worked on her boat with those deft, nimble human fingers. But I'd known that I couldn't stay the night. Too many people would look for me now that I was valuable.

As I entered my cave, the sounds of the feast penetrated through the walls: laughter, the clink of cups, squeals and shouts. I wondered if Havamal had gone back to the feast or to his room to lick his wounds alone. The king would expect him to choose someone. I was sure that even now the other guards were plotting to set him up with someone. In his position, how long would he delay before he chose another mermaid?

Pushing aside the kelp curtain, I swam into the enclosed closet. I pulled out the aged wooden chest that I kept to store the human things I collected. It was the only human object Mama had ever given me. She'd dragged it back from one of the wrecks herself, to cheer me up when Havamal joined the King's Guard and stopped coming every day to see me.

I unfastened Ragna's necklace and put it back in the chest. Tonight of all nights, when my refusal to pick a mate spat in the king's face, I could scarcely afford to get caught wearing a human pendant. Wearing it before had been reckless, maybe stupidly so. Yet the rough metal against my skin made me feel like a well-traveled shell, something swept along the seabed until it reached our desolate corner of the ocean—a reminder that somewhere beyond the reaches of the ice, there was more.

"You're back." Mama's voice came from the other side of the curtain and made me jump. "Finally. When you didn't show up at the feast, I started to get worried. All the other girls were talking about you."

"I bet they were," I muttered. Hastily, I threw everything back into the chest before sweeping the curtain aside. Even though Mama knew about the treasures I kept and had given me the chest, she still looked pained when she caught me examining them. "I didn't feel like going to the feast. I went for a swim."

She nodded and curled her fins under her to sit on my bed. I took a seat beside her, and she placed a delicate coral comb in my lap. "Havamal brought that round about an hour ago. Said he made it himself."

Wrinkling my nose, I resisted the urge to throw the comb through the cave's mouth into the open sea. Each point had been delicately carved and shaped, with no sharp edges to catch or pull my hair. Along the top, Havamal had engraved tiny human boats, bobbing on a jagged line of waves. He must have spent days making this. I swallowed hard. It was perfect, and that made it all the more awful.

"You were probably right to get away," Mama continued. She plucked the comb from my fingers and slipped it into my hair. "Six girls didn't pass this year. There were fights among the boys."

My breath caught. Havamal had mentioned Vigdis, but who were the others? Six. Every year for the past decade, fewer and fewer girls had passed the mage's test. Some whispered that the next would be our last generation unless we moved. I crossed my arms over my stomach. If it came to it, would the king force me?

"Havamal came after me today," I whispered. The comb seemed to burn against my scalp. "He followed me to that wreck we used to go to as kids. You know, the one just past the estuary."

Mama nodded. "He told me what happened there."

He'd told my mother? That seemed like a betrayal, too. Havamal had known Mama all his life, but the things we'd said to each other in the ship should have stayed private.

"I don't know what to do." My voice wobbled, and boiling tears made me wince as they burned my cheeks. "Have you ever wished you could leave? Have you ever wished there was somewhere else we could go?"

She shrugged and picked up a stray piece of netting from my floor. "My job as weaver isn't unbearable. But there's pressure on you I never had to face. In my year, only one failed. It was hard when your father died, but now I'm old enough that no one considers me as a possible mate."

"Will the king... will he make me?" I asked. The fear of being forced felt like a thousand shark teeth closing on my heart. But with six failures... Mama had wanted me to talk to the mage about going to the sea god's court. I'd feared that would be swapping one bad situation for another, but maybe I should have done it. After all, I didn't know life at Aegir's court would be miserable.

Mama pulled me closer. Her jaw stiffened. "Not while I'm living."

I leaned my head against her shoulder, but, even as her words reassured me, a knot twisted in my stomach. If I were anything

69

like Ragna, I'd stand up to the king instead of fantasizing about the day I could make my escape. I'd fight him, rather than rely on my mother's protection.

Sitting up again, I tugged Havamal's comb from my hair and studied it. The rows of boats taunted me. Once upon a time, I'd thought Havamal would carve out my future as easily as he'd etched his flawless design into the coral. Maybe that was why I resented him so much now. Day by day, he built a future for himself in a place that would turn me into a prisoner. I needed to do something to ensure my own future instead of relying on everyone else to build a life for me. *Don't be afraid to jump*, Ragna had said, and she was right. I just wished I knew where to leap.

Six

IN THE MORNING, I AWOKE to silence in the glacier. The usual hum of people starting the day was absent. Doubtless, everyone was still sleeping after yesterday's feast and the drinking that always followed. Swinging my fins carefully off my shelf, I moved like a ghost to the wooden chest. I knew that drinking sometimes made people extra sensitive to noise, and life was easier when everyone ignored me.

I opened the chest and took out the two objects that fascinated me most: an oblong bone, hollowed and decorated with silver, and a metal ring far too big for my bicep, open at one side and pierced with holes. No matter how often I looked at these objects, I could never understand what a human would use them for. My heart sped up with glee; my fingers danced over the silver engravings. Today, I would finally find answers and with them, some insight into other worlds.

For my last birthday, Mama had made me a satchel with weaving so tight that even water couldn't pass between the strands of kelp. I stuffed the human objects inside, concealing the gleaming silver from view. Then I swam into the crisp morning sea. The water near the surface was fresh and soft from the falling rain. With less of the harsh salt that dried my fins, the rainwater was a gentle caress. I spread my arms, trying to feel the water on as many parts of my body as I could.

During a storm, the seals always hid in their snow lairs, so the birds swam brazenly around the edges of the glacier. Just overhead, I could see the undersides of seabirds, floating like tiny ships bobbing on the waves. The birds' spindly legs propelled them as they looked for fish drawn to the surface by the splashing of the raindrops.

Chuckling to myself, I blew a stream of air upward. The seagulls flapped their wings, fighting with each other to attack the ripple that broke the surface.

Most of the belugas were sleeping when I reached their surfacing point. The whales lolled from side to side near the surface, drifting as the motion of the sea pushed them. I slipped between them as carefully as I could, trying not to brush against them. One of the juveniles nuzzled me sleepily as I passed him, and I stopped to rub his chin. With a twinge of sadness, I realized that if I left, with or without Havamal, I'd miss these whales more than any of the merfolk in the glacier—except Mama.

I hoisted myself over the lip of the ice. The winds were strong today and ice dust blew into my eyes. Squinting into the horizon, I saw that Ragna had begun work on her sea craft. A small boat was upside down with the hull facing the sky. Nothing remained of her makeshift shelter and, for a gut-wrenching moment, I wondered if the rain had washed her into the sea.

Leaving my satchel at the edge of the water, I scrambled toward the hull on my belly. Jagged ridges of ice nicked my fins, but I pulled myself forward anyway. There was a gap between the rim of the boat and the surface of the ice. I flattened myself on my stomach and peered in. Eyes tightly shut, Ragna was huddled amongst her belongings. Her clothes and furs were soaked through, and her skin looked gray with frost. Even in sleep, she shivered. Her slender form looked more fragile than ever. How long had she been this cold?

Grunting with effort, I lifted the hull and slipped under. Even half-dead with cold, Ragna moved faster than I could blink. Freezing metal pressed against the back of my neck. She studied me in the dimness before lowering her knife with a shuddering breath. "Sorry. I just reacted…"

With a shiver, I wondered when she had learned to sleep with a knife beneath her head. Swallowing hard, I nodded, folding my tail inside the little ship before lowering it over us. "Why are you under here?"

Ragna blew into her pale hands so her hot breath formed mist. "The rain. I kept building most of the night, just so I wouldn't freeze." She made a sound like the whimper of an animal being strangled. "But I can't get warm, and every time I doze off, I'm afraid I won't wake up."

I bit my lip. If I heated my scales, she could warm herself against the plates. But drawing body heat to the surface burned our fat reserves quickly, so quickly that someone might notice the change in my appearance when I returned home. She shivered and coughed into her closed fist. The cough was deep and wet, and her body shook so violently I imagined I could hear her ribs rattling. If I stayed under the boat, I could get caught. With the result of my grading, the king would relish any chance to arrest me. But if I didn't warm her, she might die.

I closed my eyes before flexing the micro-tendons that ran along the underside of my scales. The action hurt. My body wasn't used to performing this process, and the muscles protested as I strained. I shifted so that I was sitting entirely on her furs. Without a barrier, I worried that I might melt a hole in the ice beneath us.

Each turquoise scale along my tail warmed as if the sun had struck it. My heart beat faster; my breathing came in abrupt gasps as if I were swimming as fast as I could. "Here, press yourself against me."

Ragna's eyebrows shot up. "What?" she asked warily.

"Against my scales. It'll warm you," I said, gritting my teeth against the muscle fatigue that threatened to overwhelm me. I would need to eat—soon.

She shifted so that her weight rested against my side and then drew back with a yelp. "You're burning…"

I nodded. "We draw heat from the sun. Our scales act as plates to bring it in and store it. We can also push heat out, but it tires us."

Ragna pressed herself against me. Her body felt amphibian: cold and moist, slick with melting ice. But there was something nice about it, too, like the way her frosted cheek felt when she rested it against my shoulder and the way her hair fanned across my back. I couldn't remember when I'd held someone like this. She smelled of earthy things and taunted my curious nose with a fragrance that was at once delicate and gamy. What did I feel like to her? What did the sea smell like to a creature of land? Did she resent my cold breath?

A flush warmed my face, and I studied my hands. Now that the scales were heated, I relaxed my muscles. My body slumped in boneless exhaustion. When I looked at Ragna, she had fallen asleep. Smiling to myself, I pulled the furs around us to make a cocoon of heat. Under the covers, her fingers found mine in sleep. That was nice too, even if a curious electric tingling crawled up my arms at her touch. I wondered if that was part of the magic of her tattoos. Her body gave off its own warmth that flooded the space between us.

Alone together, snuggling with a girl who had held a knife to my throat only moments ago and had tried to spear me when we first met, I felt, strangely, safer and more at ease than I had in weeks. I closed my eyes and allowed my thoughts to drift.

A GROWL JOLTED ME FROM my sleep. Beside me, Ragna stirred and groggily raised an eyebrow. Then something shook the boat's hull. I peered under the tiny crack between the ice and the roof of our makeshift shelter. Silver claws and white fur glimmered in the bright daylight. A long, white snout sniffed along the ice.

My heart stopped beating. I was too far from the water. On land, I was slow and defenseless, especially now that I'd drained so much energy to heat my scales. As fragile and skinny as they looked, at least Ragna's human legs could run on the land. If the polar bear flipped the boat, I would be an easy, blubbery meal for him: slow and totally unable to flee. Polar bears did not respect the merfolk. They lived most of their lives outside our domain, and they didn't fear repercussions from us. The ice bears were known to scoop playing children from the sea's surface and devour them without a second thought. They were strong enough to drag an adult beluga from the sea. We all knew better than to get too close.

Ragna's eyes narrowed. Her muscles tensed. Then she fished for something below her feet. She grabbed a sword in one hand and her dagger in the other. Before I could stop her, she flipped the boat over with all her strength and caught the surprised bear across the jaw with the wooden hull.

As I lay writhing like a breached whale on the slippery ice, Ragna ran at the ice bear. She used the ice to her advantage, sliding toward the hulking white beast at speed. She moved like a streak of blonde lightning, flashing through the daylight like Thor with her weapon held high. I had never seen anyone move that way: swift and fearless. Ragna was terrifying. Despite the size and weight of the bear that stalked toward her, dripping blood from its injured mouth, she faced it. Where had she learned to fight like that? She had said her father gave up the idea of finding a mate for her as soon as he realized she could fight. How many of her kidnappers had she wounded before they managed to take her?

The bear circled her, paying no attention to me as I crawled on my belly toward the water. I didn't want to leave her to spar alone, but, out of the water, what could I do? The bear would finish me with one bite from its powerful jaws. If Ragna had to worry about me, it would only slow her down.

Ragna pivoted, and the beast lunged for her. The bear's jaws snapped on air, and she danced around him as the sword gleamed in the sunlight. The bear changed again, roaring with frustration. Polar bears hunted seals, belugas… prey that were as helpless and slow on land as I was. The creature wasn't used to Ragna's speed. He stumbled. With a cry, she jumped at him and plunged her sword just under the bear's injured jaw. When she wrenched the blade out, fresh, steaming blood gushed onto the ice.

Ragna tossed her sword aside. I grimaced as she wiped the bear's splattered blood from her face with the edge of a tattered sleeve. Then she stumbled toward me. Her legs were clumsy now that the danger of the fight was over and her battle-fever had ebbed.

Tearing her cloak from her shoulders, she spread it out across the ice and then collapsed onto it. Her nimble fingers pushed her ripped trousers down her hips and thighs. I stared, unable either to move to help or to look away. Those ethereal blue-ink tattoos ran down her legs and across the small of her back. Between the lines of ink, Ragna's flesh looked as soft and delicately pink as a new pearl. Her legs were long and lean, but hard muscle ran the along the backs of her calves.

She ripped off the corner of her tunic with her teeth, then tried to use the piece to bind the wound on her leg. Watching her wrap the bleeding scratch snapped me out of my daze. I slid toward her on my stomach. She wiped snot on her sleeve and shivered in the arctic air. Sweat froze along her hairline.

I took the strip of cloth. Then I laid my arm across the open wound. Ragna watched me warily, but she didn't pull away. We'd saved each other and now shared the blood debt: a promise and a bond as old as Asgard itself. Nobody had ever risked their life for me. I wouldn't forget it. I focused all my energy on the scales that ran up my bicep. They heated at my command, growing as hot as the sun for a fraction of a second.

Ragna threw her head back and screamed. Steam rose from her leg, but the injury closed. Biting back tears, she ran her bloody fingers over the new pink scar.

She leaned against my shoulder and we rested together. Our breath formed clouds in the frozen air; our heartbeats slowed until they beat as one steady drum.

At the fortress later that day, I headed straight for the food stores. Every part of my body felt shriveled and desperate for sustenance. My scales had burned through a good portion of my fat reserves. I'd need a few days of eating well to build them up again. The position of the sun indicated noon, but I couldn't face the dining hall. Other than Mama and Havamal, I hadn't spoken to anyone in the glacier since the grading ceremony.

I smiled at the two guards as I made my way into the coral comb store, but one of them stopped me with a hand on my arm. "Don't lead him on, lass," he growled as his deep cobalt eyes drilled into me. "He's smitten with you. Won't even look at the other girls. You have someone else in mind?"

I wrenched my arm away and cradled it against my chest. I didn't have to ask whom he was talking about. "That's between me and Havamal. It's none of your business."

The other guard snorted. "Like hell it isn't. He's been totally useless. Just moping around his cave. Everyone can tell how upset and distracted he is. Besides, with fertility being what it is… it's the whole clan's business now."

I pressed my lips together. Though we were no longer close, I hated the idea of Havamal in so much pain. "Havamal and I have talked about it. It's our decision. Excuse me." I pushed past them into the catacomb.

At our vault, I seized an eel tail and devoured it. I'd never experienced hunger this intense. Then I pulled a crab-dusted shark fin from one of the shelves, leaned back against the frozen wall, and gnawed as my eyes rolled in pleasure. What did I need a mate for, when there was food like this? The question made me giggle despite the guards' comments about Havamal. If everyone knew he was waiting for me, I might have less time before the king got involved.

Thinking about King Calder made me eat and eat until my stomach churned. The methodical chewing kept me breathing as I imagined the king passing me on to one of his favorites, turning over my freedom as casually as he bestowed gifts of pearls. The food was a lifeline, so I chewed even as my jaw ached. Could that happen? Surely it went against all of our laws and the word of the gods. But if six girls had failed... I bit into a crab leg and sucked the meat from its spindled claw.

A trail of heat drifting from the next catacomb caught my attention. I swam to look, hoping nothing had fallen and injured whomever was inside. Our caverns were often precariously stacked and the shelves themselves were easily broken. When I peered into the storage compartment, I saw Vigdis pressed against the wall. She held a bowl filled with carefully arranged and cut pieces of salmon, drowned in a stew of mashed oysters and scallops. Her normally cherubic face was drawn and thin. She stared into the food without moving and bit on a lock of her hair to stifle the sound of her crying. Unsure of what to say, I hovered with my hands on my hips.

When she looked up at me, Vigdis's face twisted in rage and anguish. "Did you come here to gloat? Are you making fun of me?" she screamed. "Get out! Get away from me."

"I didn't…" I stammered. "I just heard you… Look, I don't want any of it."

"Oh. I'm so happy you don't want to be lucky. I'm happy you don't want what we all do—that makes it all so much better!" Her voice dropped to a hiss and she threw the bowl at my head.

I dodged and the bowl clipped the edge of the doorframe. "Stop—"

"Get out!" Her voice had a raw, wild edge to it, like the screeches made by hungry seabirds as they dove for their competitors' eyes.

Seven

I swam beside the little boat's hull while Ragna rowed. She'd stripped down to a lighter animal-skin tunic and left most of her thick furs behind on the ice shelf. The garment was tight against her slender form, and I could see the muscles in her back and arms flex every time the oar plunged through the water. Ragna's skin was supple; it stretched and quivered in a way my less flexible scales couldn't. The polar bear's hide, scrubbed clean in the ocean water and as white as fresh snow, rested across her knees. I drifted on my on back and watched her in utter fascination.

"I need to test it," she said, cheeks flushed with exercise. She winked at me. "If it starts to sink, I'm depending on you to save me."

I chuckled, thumping my tail against the hull of the boat. "It feels pretty wobbly to me. I think you should rethink this whole boat-building thing. You're obviously terrible at it. Don't make it a career. Scary warrior maiden suits you better."

"My village was renowned for its craftsmanship."

"That doesn't say anything about you personally."

She grinned, then pretended to scowl and reached over the side of the boat to splash a handful of water at me.

"Do you realize how pointless it is to splash a mermaid?" I laughed, kicking water back at her with my tail. "I'm already wet. I live in the water."

Ragna ducked to avoid the spray and stuck her tongue out. Since she'd warmed herself on my scales the day before, her wariness seemed to have melted away. Thinking about it, I realized that a lot of my own reservations were gone as well.

"I'm not sure you could drag me. I'm heavier than I look, you know."

"I think I've proven my swimming strength well enough," I said.

She nudged me with the edge of her oar. "I can't believe how fast you are. I'm out of breath, and you're just floating along like an otter."

I rolled my eyes and stretched my arms out above my head, floating like the dead and letting the waves take me.

With a tired sigh, she dropped the oars into the bottom of the boat. The little craft bobbed in the water beside me. Then, from beneath her feet, she picked up the bone with silver plating that I'd left behind the previous day. "You should be nicer to me if you want to learn what this does."

I leaned on the edge of the boat, watching as she polished the object with the edge of her sleeve. Then she lifted it to her mouth and blew. A low, loud sound emitted from the end of the bone's curled tip. It was so resonant that it made the water around us vibrate.

"It's a hunting horn. We carry them when we go looking for game. The sound travels, so the rest of the hunting party can find the person who blows it. Some countries use them for war as well, but in my clan…" She bit her lip, as if the memory stung her as sharply as a jellyfish. "Well, we didn't want the enemy to know we were there. We hunted in silence."

Ragna handed the horn to me, and I pressed the end to my lips as she had done. The horn shook in my hand as I blew, blasting out a sound that echoed off the ice-capped mountains.

"How did they take you?" I asked hesitantly, dropping the horn back into the bottom of the boat. "You're a fighter. If your clan could hunt in silence together… well, it sounds like you were trained."

She shrugged; her expression was distant and cold. "Even warriors have to sleep. We weren't at war. Things had been peaceful for years, and our sentries were lazy. They attacked us when we were in our beds. There was chaos everywhere. Everyone was too busy trying to defend their own houses, their own families… we couldn't organize."

"And you? How did they take you?"

"They came to my house first, and one of them snuck in through the side window. But they got it wrong and they went to my brother's room, instead of where my sisters and I slept." She shook her head, and her hair fell across her face. "I heard him scream. I thought it was a night terror, so I grabbed a candle instead of a sword."

We both fell silent, just listening to the waves as they lapped against the boat's hull. I couldn't ask her if she'd seen her brother die.

Clearing her throat, Ragna retrieved the heavy metal bangle from my treasure collection. "You're not going to understand this."

"Why?" I demanded, rocking her boat until she nearly slipped overboard. "I understood about the horn."

"Because you won't even know what a horse is."

"We have horses," I said defensively. I didn't like feeling ignorant, and it wasn't as though she knew anything about the sea. "Sometimes the hunting parties catch them if they go a little farther south."

Tossing her head back, she cackled with laughter. "No. Land horses look nothing like sea horses. They're beasts the height of polar bears but a lot narrower. We ride them."

I wrinkled my nose at her. They rode on animals? Weren't they afraid the horses would turn and eat them? Polar bears were vicious, as we'd seen only the day before. They didn't respond to kindness. Many of my whale friends bore scars from their claws. "You ride… creatures of that size?"

"Horses are harmless. They just eat plants." She covered her mouth to suppress the laughter. "This is a shoe for them."

"A shoe?"

She held up her foot and pointed to the leather garment enclosing it. "Like this, it protects their feet."

"How do they wear it?"

"We nail them on." She pointed to the small holes around the edge of the bangle. "See these holes? They had nails in them once."

I drew back. "That's barbaric. You nail something into a living creature?"

No wonder these land horses served them. They were terrified into submission! I could only imagine the pain the creatures must endure while the shoes were fitted, never mind the agony of walking afterward. Under such conditions, maybe even polar bears could be ridden.

Shaking her head, Ragna sighed. "They have hard shell around their feet… like… a turtle. They don't feel the nails."

My skepticism must have showed on my face because she splashed another handful of water at me. "Don't ask questions if you won't like the answers."

"How do I know I won't like the answers until I ask the questions?"

The sun peered from behind a thick cloud, and Ragna's grin spread all the way to her ears. Sighing as the warm sun hit my scales, I rested my weight on the edge of the boat. Out here, out in the open water joking with her, I felt totally free. I didn't want to think about when this day would end and I'd have to swim home.

Ragna watched me as I sunned myself; her eyes were acutely focused on my face. I tried to not flush at the feral light in her eyes.

"You should give me a kiss," she said, wiggling her eyebrows. "When the bards tell mermaid stories, it's always supposed to lucky for sailors to kiss them."

"Oh, really?" I asked, trying to sound calm, though my voice came out like a squeak. My vision made a tunnel, and the only thing I could focus on was the brilliant red of her lips. Did she mean a proper kiss? Or a peck on the forehead like Mama gave me? Havamal and I had kissed a couple of times, concealed inside one of our sunken wrecks. And once, just once, I'd shared a moment with a mermaid named Fryen before Vigdis turned her against me, too. Mermaids were encouraged to kiss and make love to each other—the king condoned anything that made us more receptive to touch.

Somehow I didn't think kissing a human would be anything like that. The thought made my breathing shallow. "And why is that?"

"Mermaids are said to be the most beautiful creatures in Midgard." She shrugged. "But maybe the sailors who find them were just lucky to begin with."

"Are said?" I raised my own eyebrow in an attempt at disdain.

"Are." Ragna said. She leaned toward me, and my heart beat faster. It was just going to be a quick kiss, why was I getting so worked up? "And I'm going to need a lot of luck."

She brushed her silken lips across mine. The bitter smell of the sea clung to her now, mixed with the earthen sweetness that was her own. The sensation of her warmth shot down my back. She moved to pull away, but I wrapped my hands around her and crushed her lips to mine. The taste of her was like an elixir of salt and courage and freedom. I couldn't get enough. Some animal part of my brain insisted that I needed more.

Her fingers began working their way into my hair, threading between the layers, massaging my scalp. Her tongue teased my mouth open and slipped inside. I couldn't help the moan that escaped. She pushed against me with exactly the right amount of pressure; her lips were a thousand times softer and more agile than Havamal's had been. We kissed and kissed until I couldn't breathe, until my lips stung.

I pushed myself higher up the side of the craft. I wanted to crawl inside with her, to wrap my body around her and feel her downy skin beneath my fingers. Only the potential indignity of needing her to roll me from the boat kept my tail in the water.

I didn't know what the kiss meant. I knew she was leaving to find whatever destiny awaited her in a place I couldn't go. I wasn't sure if this was the kind of kiss she'd had in mind. In the moment, it didn't matter. The pure pleasure was enough. We were just two beings, adrift in the open ocean. Our hair whipped wildly around us, a billowing sail of blue and white.

I was equal, alive, free.

MY EYES FLUTTERED OPEN AT the sound of a single word: "Stop!"

Ragna's lips were still locked against mine. Her hot breath tickled the hollow of my neck. How could I stop, when it felt so perfect?

"Stop!"

I spun around so quickly Ragna nearly fell over the boat's edge into the sea. She scrambled to right herself in the boat as I turned to stare at the source of the commands.

Havamal treaded water an orca-length away. When our eyes met, he crossed the distance between us with a single kick of his muscular tail. His gaze flitted from me to Ragna. There was a heat in his eyes, a building pressure of rage and horror that pulsed behind the icy mask of his features like an undersea volcano. I'd never seen him look like that.

"What are you thinking?" he yelled, taking me by both shoulders and shaking me. "A human? You're kissing a human?"

"It was nothing, just a kiss—" I tried to say, but was it? My mouth still tasted of her; my lips still burned. I wanted to kiss her again. I felt like myself with her, my real self. It wasn't love, but it wasn't nothing either.

Mocking laughter erupted from him. "Just a kiss? Just a kiss, she says. Oh, yeah, just casually kissing a bloody human. Where did you even find her, Ersel?" He shook his head. "Gods, was *that* your stupid plan for us? Go on an adventure and meet some humans? Maybe join their whaling parties? You seem to have forgotten: you have fins!"

Growling, he released my shoulders and pushed me away. He rounded on Ragna's boat and shoved his full body weight into the side. The wood held fast, but the hull tipped almost enough to send Ragna into the sea. Panic seized me. We were too far from land. If she fell in the water here, she'd freeze. And if she survived the cold, would Havamal drown her?

As if in answer to my question, Havamal backed up to gather speed. Ragna fished a spear from under her feet and held it up. The metal glinted in the sun. Havamal just laughed. But it was a cruel laugh, without any humor, and the knot of fear inside me tightened. After seeing her fight the polar bear, I wasn't sure who would win this battle. The water was Havamal's domain, but Ragna was lightning made flesh. Worse, I wasn't sure which of them I wanted to win.

I grabbed Havamal about the waist. "Don't you dare," I screamed, finding my voice at last.

"It's my orders," he said, trying to shake me off. "If we see a human, we're to kill it. By order of King Calder."

"Stop it!" I was unable to keep the plea from my voice. He was much bigger and stronger than I was, and there was only so long I could hold him back. "It was only a kiss. I just wanted to try it." I said the words to placate him. When I glanced up at Ragna with her wild hair, her white fingers clutching at her spear, her lips still wet from my kiss, I felt as if I were the one he was drowning.

Some of the anger left him, and he stopped struggling. He turned to me and said in a flat voice, "Say that you'll be my mate, and I'll let her go."

If I refused, he would drown her or die trying. I could see the resolve in the rigid set of his shoulders. Would he make me watch while he held her under? Or would he drag me away, leaving her to the mercy of the frozen sea? I thought of the bodies sinking into the abyss of the cold gray ocean after the shipwreck.

"Havamal, please," I begged. Restrained tears and snot clogged my voice. "We were friends. Please. You know I don't want that. You promised you'd never force me."

"You promised me there was no one else," he whispered, and for a second I thought his voice would break, but his eyes were hard as stone.

"Please."

"No. Come or I knock her out of the boat."

"All right." I slumped. I'd always argued that Vigdis was wrong, that nothing inside me was frozen. But now defeat chilled me to the core, wrapping its fingers around my heart, turning it black. I could not watch him kill her. "I'll do it. I'll come with you."

"Don't you dare try to go back on it," he warned. "Or I'll tell everyone about the human. And they'll believe me."

They would. We both knew it. I kept to myself, and no one would support my word above his. If Havamal told the court that I had not only aided, but also befriended and… kissed…

a human, the king would peel all the scales from my back and leave me to die on the ice shelf.

"I said I would do it." I would try to plead later. There was no way my best friend had turned into someone so cruel. He was angry and hurt. It would pass and he'd change his mind.

Havamal nodded, then tugged on my arm. "Let's go."

"Let me say goodbye."

He heaved a sigh and then sank under the waves. I could make out his shadow, lurking just below my tail fins. Ragna would think he had gone, that we were alone. But I wondered if this was just the beginning. Would he watch me day in, day out, until we went through the mating ceremony? I heaved, and bile rushed up from my stomach to burn my throat with acid.

No. He was angry. That was all.

As I swam to Ragna's boat, my fins dragged as if someone had tied the anchor of a human ship to my tail. She knelt in the hull and peered into the water at me with her dazzlingly bright eyes. I wanted to kiss her. I wanted to jump in the boat and let her row us away. I wanted to escape.

Instead, I grabbed the side of the tiny ship, pulled myself up, and whispered into her ear, "Row. You have to get away from here."

"What if he comes back? He nearly tipped me." Her lips pursed. "I'm not sure the boat is ready to go out on the open water. I took my food so the gulls wouldn't get it but… what if I sink?"

I managed a watery smile. "You won't. Mermaid luck, remember?"

She winced. "It doesn't look like it's brought you very much luck."

"I don't think the legend works like that."

"I can't just leave you here… what is he going to do to you?"

I shrugged, then tried to make my voice sound confident. "I'm not sure. But we used to be friends, so maybe it will be all right."

"You don't sound convinced."

"I'm not, but he will drown you if you don't leave now."

Ragna managed a weak smile, then pressed the hunting horn back into my hands. I stared at the silver mouthpiece, imagining her lips wrapped around it. Then she said, "I will come back."

"You shouldn't," I whispered, even as my stomach did a back flip.

Her hand squeezed mine. "Are you sure you're going to be okay? Until then?"

Every part of me wanted to shout "no!" but I nodded, dropped her hand, and said goodbye.

Eight

I REFUSED TO SPEAK TO Havamal as we swam back to the glacier. He tried once to break the silence by clearing his throat, but I didn't even grunt in response. My mind raced with thoughts of Ragna. Would the water in her canteen hold out? Would she make it to the shore? Would I ever see her again? Part of me wanted to imagine her sitting in her boat, looking up at the twilight, waiting where I'd left her. In my daydreams, Havamal stopped, apologized, and let me go back to her.

But in reality, his hand remained fastened around my wrist like a chain. I half expected him to haul me before the king and make me publicly announce my intentions. Instead, he escorted me to my own cave and then hovered in the alcove, biting his lip as though he had something to say.

When I still said nothing, he shook his head and murmured, "I'll come back and check on you in an hour or so. When we've both cooled off."

"And then you'll apologize, and we can forget about this?" I rubbed the back of my head and tried to laugh even though I wanted to sob.

He frowned and gripped the edge of the ice cave to steady himself. "We can talk about when we'll tell the king." Then he swam away.

Feeling numb, I propped the horn up against the wall of my cave. I surveyed my human treasures, wondering if I should scoop them up and hurl them into the ocean so Havamal wouldn't have physical evidence to use against me. But everything inside me ached, so I curled into a ball, wrapped my tail around me, and buried my face in my fins.

Havamal had me trapped and he knew it. Whether the king believed him or not, he would take Havamal's side. By now, everyone would have heard about the ceremony. King Calder would see my body as too valuable to waste and he would make a decision based on what I could do rather than what I wanted. Would he strip my scales before he turned me over to Havamal? I tried to rest, but all I could do was imagine the king's cruel laugh as he flayed rows of scales from my back, leaving my flesh bare to the burning cold salt of the ocean water. He'd done it to others before, even to his own sister.

Shivering, I raised my eyes to the ceiling. Havamal had been my best friend and now he wanted to be my jailer—a warden disguising himself as lover, forcing me to do his bidding.

I've never been particularly pious, but praying to Loki before the ceremony had seemed to help. Or at least, it had eased my anxiety even if the god of lies had had nothing to do with the ceremony's outcome. I didn't like the idea of adopting the trickster as my patron god, but if ever I needed a trick or two, it was now. The words of a remembered prayer tumbled from my lips. Everything inside me felt too frozen to make up my own plea.

Blue light shimmered against the back wall of my cave. It was pale and strangely electric and reminded me of watching lightning strike the sea from fifteen arm-lengths below. I swam to my crevice's mouth. Peering out into the gray water, I squinted at the source of the strange glow. The light became so intense I had to look away. It radiated from a little ball I could hardly see. All of a sudden, it blinked and dimmed. A green and yellow sea turtle glided toward me. The electric blue light glowed from his eye sockets, and he stared right at me. A shiver ran up my back, and my blood cooled.

Above me, the patter of hail echoed through the ocean, followed by the crack of lightning. I wondered if I should scream for help. Was stress making me imagine things? Sea turtles couldn't survive here, could they? With their cold blood, they needed the summer currents to survive. I shook my head to clear the image, blinked, but the turtle still swam toward me. If I screamed and there was no turtle, the king would think I was losing my mind, and I'd have less chance of defending myself against the things Havamal could say. Plus, I didn't want to wake Mama. I took a deep breath. My heart felt raw and exposed, blistered and stinging, like a wound cleansed with ocean salt. I wasn't ready to talk to her.

The turtle drifted peacefully toward me, like a moving lullaby propelled by the tide. The creature's bright eyes dimmed further, and it cocked its head, winking at me as it coasted through a school of silver fish. Then it began to paddle rapidly; its thick flippers pumped faster and faster until its whole body became a green blur. Overhead, the hail and thunder intensified—almost as if Thor himself surfed across the waves. A bolt of lightning struck the sea and a fiery purple and yellow aurora of fiery diffused over the waves.

When I looked up toward the lights, the turtle slammed into me, knocking me back into the cave. Before I could scream, a hand covered my mouth: a hand that was pink, warm, and strangely dry.

As my screams died in my throat, the creature spun me around to face them. Their turtle shell had transformed into a billowing cloak of sparkling greens and golds. Caribou antlers covered with strips of fur stuck out on either side of a silver helmet; each antler was tall enough to scrape the ceiling of my little cave. Blue, electric light emanated from their very skin. A sea snake the color of dying coral wound about their waist. I couldn't decide if I was looking at a man or a woman. Their form was slim and elegant, androgynous, with neither soft curves nor rippling muscle. High cheekbones and pursed midnight-blue lips set off hooded, bright eyes, deep-set in their chiseled face.

I wanted desperately to swim away from them, to hide behind my kelp curtain, but they gripped my shoulders so hard I could feel bruises forming under my scales.

"Do you know who I am?" they demanded, raising a turquoise eyebrow.

The blue light shining from them made my scales glow as if I lay under the sun. A bubble of dry air formed in the ice cave and expanded until it filled the space. A warm feeling crept up from the tip of my tail, even while my stomach sank in fear. The horns reminded me of images from our legends that had been carved into the ice sculptures decorating our central hall. The statues in the hall had frozen their stories into our collective memories.

I swallowed. I was seeing the same face I'd seen every day since I was a child, engraved above me in the dining hall.

Loki, god of lies. I'd memorized their crystal smirk. But their eyes now carried an animation, a mischief that matched their hardened grin.

"You're Loki," I whispered. Why would the trickster god choose to help me? This was only the second time in my life I'd prayed to them. From everything I'd heard about Loki, my situation should have amused them. Maybe they were here to taunt me, to mock me for praying to them concerning a ceremony I didn't care about and wasting whatever favor my birth season entitled me to.

They nodded, but their eyes never left my face.

"Are you here to mock me?" I asked, my voice trembling. It wasn't a polite thing to ask a god, but after what I'd been through today, I didn't have energy left for courtesy.

Laughing, Loki shook their great horned head. Their cackle was high and cruel, but then their eyes softened into something that seemed like affection. That look of care on their pale face was even more terrifying. They rested their warm hand on my back. I imagined their nails filled with poisonous venom and pulled away to avoid getting their toxin on my scales.

But Loki only smiled. "I've been watching you for a while, Ersel. It's not normal for your kind to interact so closely with the human world. You're curious and intelligent and you don't follow orders like a sheep. I value all those things."

I didn't know what a sheep was, but I nodded at the compliment nonetheless.

Their fingers played with the edges of their blue and gold eyebrow. "I want to make a deal with you."

My scales stood up on my back. Whenever the storytellers talked about Loki, they cautioned against making deals with the god. I cursed myself for carelessness, for letting Havamal follow me. If I hadn't been such an idiot, maybe I wouldn't have to decide between displeasing the god standing in front of me or doing what all our legends warned against: making a deal with the being who invented the lie.

"What is the deal?" I asked, wringing my hands.

"One wish. Anything you want. Truly, anything," they insisted, noticing my raised eyebrows. Their aura turned silver, flashing as they grew excited.

"What do I have to do?"

"I need a voice." They took a little vial from their coat and held it out. Inside, a glowing white liquid splashed against the glass. "A voice from a merperson. I can't talk to the other creatures in the sea without it. Everyone knows I can change my form at will but… voices I have to collect."

My hand went to my throat, then crept down to my belly. Was that why they had helped me at the ceremony? Did they want me to give them all the voices I carried inside me? Or my own?

"Not yours. I'm not a fool and I know you'd never give that up." They patted my shoulder again, and I recoiled. The dryness of their skin felt like sand trapped between my scales. "And the ones you carry… I know what you're thinking, but they're not voices. Not yet. They're just potential. But there must be others—an old woman perhaps? A silent maid? A merperson who would not miss their voice anyway? Who would be happier left mute and in peace?"

I couldn't think of anyone like that, but I nodded anyway. Who could be happier living the rest of their life with no voice? I couldn't imagine how isolating that would be.

"Tell me what you want to do," I said, lowering myself to sit on the edge of my pallet. "I'm not saying I'll do it; I just want to hear what the conditions would be."

To escape the situation Havamal had put me in, I was willing to listen to anything. If I could just escape, I could vanish into the ocean. I would catch up with Ragna, and who knew after that? I could find a new world.

Loki's grin widened. They stepped forward and hung the vial from a cord of twisted fibers around my neck.

LOKI VANISHED, AND THE WATER flooded back into the cave, leaving me dizzy with nervousness. I didn't know when Havamal would return or how long I had spent negotiating with the trickster, but I knew I had to hurry if I was to succeed before I was dragged in front of the king.

I slipped from my cave into the labyrinth of halls and storage bays. I didn't know if my plan would work, but there was only one mermaid I could think of who might accept Loki's conditions. Soon, I was in a less familiar part of the fortress—the most luxurious part—where each individual cave was a crystal palace of ice with its own dining chamber and sitting room. Mama and I never won numbers high enough for one of these residences, nor would we ever. Everyone knew the system was rigged. With Mama refusing to take another mate after the death of my father, and me being, well... strange and, before The Grading, undesirable, to say the least... our chances had never been good.

If I were staying, maybe we'd be allocated something better next year, since the results of the fertility ceremony made me valuable. Something tickled the back of my throat. What would Mama do, once I was gone? Would the king hold her responsible for my departure? But with my former best friend about to make me a prisoner, I couldn't let myself dwell on that.

At the end of the twisting hall, the water warmed. I crept to the doorframe of the last cave and peered inside. I hovered in the doorway, stunned by the moment of weakness I was not supposed to see. Vigdis tilted her head back to stop the flow of misery, wiping snot on a square-cut piece of seaweed.

Part of me was taken aback. I hadn't expected to find her still crying. It had been days since the ceremony. And yet I supposed that Vigdis felt as trapped as I was now, with all her dreams stripped away. I wished our positions had been reversed. I couldn't help feeling, in that moment of prayer before The Grading when I'd asked Loki for help, that I'd somehow exchanged our fates, that I'd stolen something from her.

I knocked on the outside wall, and my fist sank into the ice. She'd cried so much her home had started to melt around her. I almost felt guilty, using her like this, but given the state she was in, maybe she'd thank me. Maybe we would both get what we wanted. "Vigdis?"

"Did you come to rub it in?" she asked, pawing at her eyes. "I get it, okay? The irony of everything. That you're fertile and I'm not. "

"There's always next year," I offered. I didn't want to be too quick with my bargain, not until she relaxed and understood that I hadn't come to mock her.

"Next year?" Vigdis gave a hollow laugh and banged her head on the wall. "I got a score of eight. *Eight.* I have eight viable follicles in my entire body. With a score that low, nobody will ever want me. I'm too much of a risk even if I get a higher count next year."

"Have you thought about doing something else? Lots of merwomen have other jobs…"

"After!" Her voice broke, and boiling tears seeped into the water. "They do things after they've proved themselves. I never learned any skills. I didn't really pay attention in our lessons. Why would I? I always knew what I wanted. What am I possibly good for now?"

"I don't know. You could work in the nurseries?" Even as I said the words, I realized how insensitive they sounded.

"Get out," she whispered. Then her voice rose into a screech. "I told you before not to bother me. I never want to see you again. Get out!"

"What if there was another way?" I asked, sitting opposite her against the back wall. Her eyes narrowed. I took a deep breath, bracing myself for what I had to do. Somewhere, Loki would be watching me. I held the little vial up to the light filtering in from above. It glowed with the same neon intensity as Loki's eyes. "What if you could make a swap and find a mate and be as fertile as any of us? What would you give for that?"

Vigdis leaned forward, studying the bottle in my hands.

"I had a visit." I pressed on, now that I had her interest, turning the vial over like a timeglass. She watched the liquid run down the glass sides with rapt attention. "The god of lies."

Vigdis scowled and scooted away from me. "You're the one who's *lying*," she spat out. "The only liar here is you. What would a god want with you? With any of us?"

"Loki's been watching me."

"And what do you do that is any way interesting?" Her eyes glittered, and she hesitated and looked again at the contents of the bottle. "I've always wondered where you go... what you do... when the rest of us bask or stay to talk in the hall. Or did you cheat? Is this how you... how you did that at the ceremony?"

Her question caught me off guard and wasn't something I wanted to answer. Even now, even after everything that had happened, some part of me didn't want Vigdis to win. I didn't want her to think she'd been right all along. But if I said no, then she might not agree to give me what I needed now. I swallowed my pride and forced myself to say, "Yes."

Her eyes narrowed further, and then she pointed an accusing finger at me. "I knew it. I knew that with how you neglect yourself..."

I cut her off. "Do you want to hear the rest of what I have to say or not?"

She gave the tiniest of nods.

"I want to leave this place and make my fortune as far away from this glacier as I can. I've always wanted to leave and, until this year, I always thought that Havamal would go with me. That's over, but... I met... a human. Someone I can see the world with."

Vigdis gasped and her tears stopped. "The king will kill you."

"He can't know."

"Humans are dangerous, Ersel. They're vicious. They're scavengers. We all know that!"

I grimaced. "She's not like that—"

"She?" Vigdis snapped. "You've gotten to know her? Is she still here? Where are you hiding her? Oh, King Calder will take all your scales. He'll scrape you down until there is nothing left. And you'll deserve it. You've exposed us."

I closed my eyes as hot fear coursed through me. I'd misjudged her, and now I would pay for it. "It's not like that. She doesn't know much."

Vigdis's sharp eyes traveled back to the bottle in my hands. Her hands massaged her abdomen and the empty womb beneath her scales. A small smile twitched at the corner of her mouth. I always thought Vigdis was stupid, but it dawned on me now that she had said those things to rebalance the situation. She was used to having the upper hand with me and she wanted her power back. "You say there is another way? What way?"

"A trade."

"What could I have that the god of lies would want? I'm not even from Loki's season." She glanced around her cave and then laughed. "My pearls? My ice sculptures? Surely there are better out there, and Loki could just take them if it's what they wanted."

"Your voice."

Vigdis's body went rigid. She pressed a hand to her throat. Then, she asked sharply, "What kind of deal is that?"

I shrugged. "It's what they offered. You know the legends. They can take whatever form they want, but they have to take voices from the willing ever since Odin sealed their true lips."

It was a legend I knew well. Odin, the All-Father, had punished Loki by sewing their lips together with magically binding thread after they deceived a group of Odin's closest commanders. When the trickster changed form, the threads were invisible and they could move their adopted mouths, but the lock on their true voice remained. Even though the god of lies had made many appeals to Odin, their crime was never forgiven. Odin did not change his mind. He never went back on his word. Forevermore, Loki would need to steal voices to accompany their many forms.

"They didn't want to take yours? Is there something wrong with your voice?" Vigdis could barely contain her sneer. "Well, I guess one part of my body must be better then, even if it's not the part I wish it was."

I tried to swallow my revulsion. She actually considered her womb more important than her voice. I had guessed that before I decided to approach her, but still, having her confirm it made my stomach churn.

When I hesitated, tears leaked from her violet eyes. The water around us grew so warm, I empathized with the fish Ragna had cooked for her dinner. I felt sorry for Vigdis and guilty for what I was about to do to her. But maybe, this way, we'd both get some of what we wanted.

When I spoke again, my tone sounded harsh, even to me. The mixture of guilt, fear, and pity I felt made me lash out. I couldn't go through with what Havamal wanted from me and this might be my only chance to escape. Being a prisoner here would kill me. "Swap it then. If it's worth it to you. Swap your voice for a healthy womb and have the role you always wanted. I'm sure Loki will even toss in a mate for you, if that's what you wish."

Vigdis looked at the other side of her cave. Her expression warmed into softness. "Yes," she said. "Yes."

When I returned to my crevice, I had no choice but to sit and wait for Loki. What if Havamal came back before the god did? Would Loki intervene? I'd fulfilled my promise to them, and even the gods were bound by their oath. I repeated the trickster's name again and again to no avail.

I supposed you couldn't call a god and expect them to answer like a trained whale. But what if they didn't come in time? What if I'd taken Vigdis's voice, and there would be no mate for her and no escape for me? The vial containing her sacrifice glowed in my hands, dangling from a rope around my neck.

I'd decided to ask for legs. Then, like a seabird or a sand crab, I could choose the land or the sea for my home. I could go anywhere. I wanted to keep my gills and possibly some of my scales too. I liked Ragna's form well enough, but since I wasn't blessed with gods-given magical tattoos, my skin would look awfully plain if it were… just bare.

Something moved in the shadows and brushed my kelp curtain aside. My heart leapt into my mouth. I saw a flash of silver fin. No. He could not have returned already. Not now. Not after what I'd just done.

But then Loki swam into full view. The bottom half of their body was replaced by a gleaning silver tail that matched Havamal's to the shade. The sea serpent around their waist hissed and unwound, slithering across the ice floor toward me.

I recoiled, lifting my hands in front of me to block it, but the snake persisted. He curled around me. His hot tongue flicked against the back of my neck. Then the twin forks of his tongue twisted around the rope attached to the vial. The snake skillfully undid the rope's knot and pulled the vial from my neck. I felt the weight lessen around my throat, the binding collar gone as well as the burden. The snake slithered away and delivered the voice to Loki's outstretched palm.

The god turned the bottle over in their long fingers and then pressed it to their face. They closed their eyes, as if the vial stroked their cheek. Then, sniffing around the cork, they said, "This will do nicely for what I have in mind."

I crossed my arms over my chest and tried to sound brave. "What are you planning to use it for?"

Loki swam toward me and patted my head. "Never you mind that, little mermaid. You've done well with this. What did she ask you for in exchange?"

"A mate." Just saying it made me ache for Vigdis, who genuinely believed she'd gotten the better deal. As she'd sung into the bottle, she'd smiled and all her tears had finally gone. "And fertility. She didn't do well at The Grading."

Loki nodded and stroked the moustache they'd grown in the hours since our previous meeting. They snapped their fingers, grinning. "Easily done."

"It was that easy?" The speed made me nervous, but then, what did I know about how the gods' powers worked?

A deep chuckle ripped from their throat. "It was not a difficult request."

"And mine?" I prompted them. My gaze darted to the entrance of the ice cave. Havamal could be back any moment, unless he'd had a change of heart. Part of me prayed that he had… but I was beyond that now, and I couldn't wait any longer. "I want legs. Will it be a difficult request? And make sure I can breathe... and not freeze. I don't want to drown down here. And I want to keep some of my scales."

"Going after your little human friend?"

I shrugged. Would I seek Ragna? Probably, if only to see if we could have a chance... if things might continue to develop between us. I didn't relish the idea of being completely alone. But if she wanted to stay on land forever, then I didn't know. I wanted the chance to explore. I wanted to see the lands beyond the ice shelves, the distant countries where human hunters like Ragna lived.

Loki's eyes lit with an emotion I couldn't quite read. Dread mixed with my excitement. What if this deal didn't turn out as I expected? But it was too late... I'd done what he asked for and given my request. It was too late to give Vigdis her voice back, even if I wanted to.

The trickster opened their mouth and swallowed the glass vial whole. Their body glowed white, then they stretched their spectral fingers toward me. I scooted forward, holding my breath. They caressed my fins, one at a time, with a sort of reverence I wasn't expecting. I imagined the long, beautiful form my legs would take. Delicate like a human's, but still bejeweled with turquoise scales. They would be strong, elegant. I could run across the land, fierce and agile on my two flawless limbs. Surely, being sculpted by a god, they would be truly perfect.

I shut my eyes as a tingling feeling spread upward. I could feel my tail splitting and growing into new shapes, but it wasn't painful. My body was like sand—malleable and soft—with just enough substance to stop it drifting away with the tide.

"It's done," Loki said.

I opened my eyes and peered down at my new body.

I had legs. But they were long and spindly, coated in slippery aquamarine skin. Little mouths ran their length. The mouths gasped before I did. I shifted, and, as my new legs touched the ice, the mouths attached to the freezing surface, sucking like hatchlings at their mother's breast.

Eight. Eight monstrous tentacles protruded below my waist where my tail used to be. They were covered in slimy film, water-based like squid skin, and would need to stay wet constantly.

When I looked up again, Loki had vanished.

Someone deep within the glacier screamed, and then more frantic shouts followed. I tried to listen to what they said, but my own howls, part terror, part agony, drowned out everything around me.

Whatever I had imagined might happen when I made a deal with the trickster god, this was worse.

Nine

WHEN MY OWN SCREAMS STOPPED, I yanked my kelp curtain down from its pins and wrapped it around myself. Then I returned to my pallet and tried to curl into a ball. But my new legs wouldn't obey, wouldn't close around me in a comforting embrace the way my tail had done. I tucked the blanket under my body and the legs rebelled, moving as if compelled by a separate mind, seeking freedom from the restraint. I prayed to Odin, Frigga, Ran, Aegir… anyone I could think of who might have the power to undo what Loki had done. But even as my lips mouthed another whispered plea, I knew my fate was sealed. I'd made the deal and in their sadistic way, Loki had honored it.

The gods would not intercede when there was an agreement.

What would the king do? Sickness gnawed at me, and I swallowed hard to keep my breakfast inside. Would he see this as a rebellion? Would I be a criminal now? Exiled to the dungeons and kept out of sight? Havamal could go to hell, but what if I weren't allowed to see Mama again?

And Ragna, how could I possible go after her like this? Even if the new legs would allow me to walk on land, I was a monster.

The other humans would hunt me. I'd die before I found her. Mermaid kisses were lucky. But who would want an abomination?

I took a deep, shuddering breath. I could starve myself until my body withered or find a way, somehow, to live with the outcome.

"Ersel?" Mama appeared at the entrance to my ice cave. Her orca-black fins swept the ice elegantly behind her. "Ersel, are you all right? I thought I heard you scream, but with everything going on outside…"

I folded the new legs as tightly as I could, smoothing the kelp over them. There was no way I could hide my new body for long, but I'd cherish these precious seconds. If the king locked me away, they might be the last ones we'd have. I cleared my throat. "What's happening outside? Is everything okay?"

Mama covered her mouth and shook her head. "It's one of your year-mates… That girl with the coral fins. Vigdis? Her mother went to visit her and found a strange merman in her chambers. She said he was handsome, beautiful even … with golden starlight fins and skin the color of midnight." Mama paused for breath. "She found them kissing, but when she arrived, they fled. She was happy for Vigdis, goodness knows the girl was miserable after the ceremony results… but when they swam away, Croa said, the merman trailed a green mist, and when she looked into it, he appeared like something else, something monstrous."

"Is she sure of what she saw?" I took a deep, ragged breath. "She must be under a lot of stress, too, after what the mage found out about Vigdis…"

Mama shrugged. "Croa has a good head on her shoulders. She wouldn't invent. She was sure."

I wasn't sure I wanted to know, but I had to ask. "What does she think she saw?"

"A creature with tusks like an elephant seal, with hooves for hands and a tail with a thousand eyes for scales." Mama's voice shook as she repeated what she'd heard.

My hand went to my throat and a creeping burn spread up it. My stomach heaved, and I vomited into the water. The orange mush drifted past me, and Mama moved aside to let it pass into the ocean.

Loki's tricks and my stupidity had punished Vigdis twofold—as if losing her voice wasn't sacrifice enough. *A mate.* My stomach churned. Maybe threefold. What if there was another punishment planted inside her, growing with every passing minute? The thought made me retch again. I coughed and heaved up pure bile. I was responsible for this.

"Do you have a fever, Erie?" Mama swam beside me and stroked my hair. Her fingers began combing through the knots, as she'd done a thousand times. Misery clogged my throat. I shut my eyes as hollowness bore through me, as if a thousand sand crabs carved out their dens inside me all at once.

"No," I stammered. "It's just ... the news."

"I know, it's sickening," Mama said, her voice gentle. "But it'll be okay. The King's Guard will find her and bring in this merman for questioning, whoever he is. She'll be safe soon. We can't be too careful when it comes to shapeshifters ... it's *haustr* and all of Loki's monsters prowl."

When I didn't reply, her eyes traveled down the netted kelp blanket. "Why are you all covered up?"

I didn't have time to respond.

Chest heaving, Havamal swam into the center of my cave. "Ersel?" he asked, voice thick with concern. Once upon a time, his concern would have made me blush with glee. Now it made me feel sicker. "I heard you scream? Did you see something?" His eyes darted around the enclosed cave. "Did you see that thing? The shapeshifter Vigdis followed? We're looking for them now ... Gods, I only hope her mother didn't see what she thought she did."

Cold rage made me unwind the kelp from around my new legs so he could see what he'd driven me to do. Free from their bondage, the tentacles pawed at the air without me guiding them. The mouths puckered and kissed the open water, looking for something solid to attach themselves to.

Mama went rigid and then started to shake. Havamal just stared.

"What...?" Mama's voice trailed off.

All the color had drained from Havamal's handsome face. Good. He should feel shame. But Vigdis... Havamal wasn't responsible for what I'd done to her.

"It's all my fault," I whimpered, breaking at last when I reached for Mama's hand, and she cringed away. I yanked the kelp back over my body, but the tentacles pushed it aside. "I made the deal. It's all my fault."

THREE OF THE KING'S OTHER guards burst into the ice cave. Doubtless they had heard my screaming as well, but as soon as their eyes fell on my tentacles and beheld what I'd become, they pounced on me. My new legs flared out against my will, striking at them and seeking something to grip.

"Stop it!" Havamal protested weakly, but he didn't move to stop them. His hand had found Mama's, and he clung to her. I hated him all the more, even if he was defending me. How dare he touch my mother after what he'd done? "She needs help. Don't hurt her."

A blue-tailed guard shook his head. "Look at her. It's obvious she's part of whatever has happened here today. Maybe she's in league with whatever beast stole the coral girl."

My tentacles splayed, catching the guard across the face so hard he staggered.

"Don't resist them, Ersel," Mama wept. "You'll make it look worse. You can explain it to the king. You were here the whole time; how could you have kidnapped that girl? It'll all be a misunderstanding. As soon as they find Vigdis, everything will be all right." She had retreated into the corner of the room and folded in on herself. For the first time in my life, she looked small.

"I'm not trying to!" I protested but my new body had a mind of its own. I felt like a toy, limp and controllable, caught in Loki's unpredictable hands.

One of the waiting guards ran at me and circled my legs in his powerful arms. I broke his grasp as if it were nothing, with a miniscule flex. Growling, the guard pulled a sharpened rock from his side satchel. He slashed it through the air, cutting into one of my tentacles. Even though the new legs didn't feel as though they belonged to me, the pain made me yelp. My legs stilled.

Working together, the guards dragged me down the hall, past the food stores, and down through the locked and enclosed brooding chambers. My lungs constricted, and I gasped for air even though my gills functioned as well as ever, just as I'd stipulated in the bargain. After everything I'd done, I was being dragged to a prison darker than the one I'd sought to avoid. Somewhere off in Asgard, Loki would laugh at the irony.

We swam farther and deeper into the heart of the glacier. The light from above dwindled, and the world became an abyss of cold black. Finally, we stopped. The guard holding my legs released me. The others flung me into a room I could not see. Then they pulled something heavy across the entrance and sealed me in the deep.

*   *   *

I DON'T KNOW HOW LONG I lay pressed against the back wall of the tiny cell. In the dark, time passed erratically. The slick coldness of the wall chilled me to the core in minutes, but I needed something solid against me. When they first threw me in the cave, I'd scrambled with my arms and tentacles outstretched. I couldn't hear or see anything, and the panic had made my bowels release.

Under most circumstances, the court wouldn't be allowed to keep me in a place like this when I hadn't begun my trial or questioning, but I supposed the sight of my uncontrolled new legs made them frightened enough to forgo the rules. Furthermore, until Vigdis was found, everyone would be on edge. Shapeshifters were rooted in our legends, and no one doubted their existence, but we all knew they were capricious creatures, compelled by the trickster's whim and every bit as volatile as the god themself.

By the time one of my tentacles slapped against the far back wall, I was hyperventilating and close to fainting. Shivering,

I nuzzled against the wall, trying to imagine that this was all a dream and soon the daylight would wake me on my resting shelf.

Then, I just lay there, letting my guilt pick away at pieces of my soul, like worms inside a corpse. I'd been so selfish. So blind.

Slowly, I lost track of time. They would have found Vigdis by now, I was sure of it, but no one came to tell me of her fate. My imagination took over, and I thought about all the things the shifter might have done to her. Sometimes our warriors told harrowing stories about the human bodies they found in the deep. They had been mutilated by their own kind before being silenced by the waves. Had Vigdis suffered a fate so brutal that no one dared speak of it to me? If she was all right, then surely someone would come ... surely someone would release me, despite my appearance.

Hours or days later, someone knocked.

Then a gruff voice shouted, "You're going to trial. The girl ..." His voice broke in a shudder. "The girl is pregnant."

Everything inside me went numb, but I managed to croak. "What day is it? How long have I been here?"

The male voice just laughed, and I was left in the dark to rot.

Pregnant. The word rang in my ears again and again. I tried not to think about Vigdis. Would she be happy or terrified? What grew inside her? What had become of the shifter who seduced her and whose discovery condemned me to this cell, deep in the ice?

Hunger gnawed at me as the days passed, but not knowing threatened to crush me whole. What had the creature done to her? Beyond the tentacles that grasped and sucked at the walls, how deep did my own monstrosity run?

I pressed myself tighter against the wall. It was so cold that the blood seemed to stop in my veins. And after days hidden from the sun's eye, I could barely summon a kernel of energy to heat my scales. I was alone and frozen and trapped in a curse of my own making.

A whisper pierced the silence. I lifted my head, straining to catch the sound and wondering if I'd imagined it. Then I heard someone shuffle and sit down.

"Ersel?" Havamal called from somewhere in the neverending darkness. His voice sounded hoarse and exhausted. "Please. Please, I'm sorry. I just want to talk."

Part of me wanted to ignore him or scream for him to leave, but I was so desperate for a friendly voice to break the murderous silence that I crawled along the floor on my belly toward the sound. Then, one of my legs brushed against the front wall, and I slid against the door. It was built from thousands of clamshells and mortared with a paste made from sand and the sticky jelly that fish secreted around their eggs.

For a second, I wondered if my new legs could break through it. But my crime was real, even if I hadn't intended it. If I didn't attend my trial, no one would ever know the truth, and my guilt would continue to eat away at me forever.

"Erie?" Havamal whispered, softer this time. I could smell him under the door; his scent was brackish: rainwater and salt and fresh-caught salmon. A second later, a purple light flashed. Havamal had brought a jellyfish to guide his way, just as he'd done when we were children.

The light illuminated the tiny crack at the bottom of the door. I lay against it, bathing in the glorious light, trying to soak it all up. I was just so cold. "I'm here," I said.

"I…" He hesitated, and the light flickered, as if he were cupping the jelly in his hands. "I never should have said I would force you. I wouldn't have. As soon as I left your room and started to cool down, I hated myself for saying it. I was just so angry when I saw you with that human girl. All I could think was that I wanted to get you away from her, but now everything is ruined. I screwed everything up."

I just listened to him in silence, holding my breath. Even so, I felt a little of the anger flow from me, to be replaced by sadness. If I'd known he wouldn't make me choose him, then everything might be different. Years ago, I would have dismissed the idea of Havamal forcing me to become his mate without a second thought. It would have seemed too cruel, too ludicrous, to accept from my best friend.

But the fact that I'd believed him, as well as the fact that he'd said it at all, showed just how much our friendship had decayed. I barely knew the person he'd become.

"Would you have drowned her?" I asked. My voice sounded creaky from disuse. "If I hadn't come with you?"

Havamal sighed. The door rocked ever so slightly as he sagged against it. "Yes."

Rage flared up again before I could stop it. "So you feel bad for making me think you would force me to be your mate, but you don't feel bad that you would have killed someone?"

"She's a human," Havamal said, and I heard the pain in his voice. "They're our enemies. They're savage. If she's been living in this place, then she may have mapped it out. Figured out a way to navigate through the ice. It's not safe to let her return to her people."

"But you let her go when I came with you."

"I want you more than I want to be safe," he whispered. "It took me until that moment, when I had to make a choice, to figure that out. If we still could, I'd leave with you right now. I'd go anywhere you wanted."

I closed my eyes as a bolt of pain coursed through me. The dream of escaping together was shattered now, and I realized I didn't want to go back to it.

If I lived through my trial, I would try to forgive him, but he wasn't the being I wanted alongside me. He wasn't the one I trusted to protect me, whose wild spirit made my dreams expand with new possibilities. Before Ragna, I'd never thought about life on land. Now I realized the world was vast and the ocean didn't have to limit me.

"I'm sorry," he said, and I felt warmth pool under the door.

"I forgive you." It wasn't true, not yet, but I felt compelled to say it because I might never get another chance. I had little doubt that the king would execute me after the trial.

We sat without talking until Havamal said, "They're going to question me before your trial. They'll ask you some preliminary questions, but…" He cleared his throat. "Even the king wouldn't dare put you on trial already marked."

"Marked?"

"You know, with scars or missing scales. It wouldn't sit well. People would say the result was faked."

I sucked in a deep breath. "But they'll do it to you?"

"King Calder knows we were close. He knows how much I wanted you." He cleared his throat, and I could almost hear the pain and shame in his words. "He'll use me to find out what happened. As far as I know."

"Will you tell them?"

"They'll get the answers they want to hear. Even if they're not the truth. One way or another," he muttered softly. Something brushed against my back, and I looked down to find one of his fingers wedged under the heavy door. It wasn't a lover's touch. Just a link between us in the abyss, proving that he was there. "No matter what they have to do. When I first started working for the king, I thought it would be an honor. The other guards are my brothers. I'm proud to fight and train with them. But the king… the king is crueler than anyone I've ever known."

I squeezed his finger. "If I have to leave…" I couldn't say die, even though it seemed inevitable. "Promise me you'll take care of my Mama?"

"Like she was my own." Then he pulled his hand back and the jellyfish's light dwindled as he swam away.

Ten

ONCE, VIGDIS AND A GROUP of her friends had cornered me after our lessons with the historian who kept the clan's records. I could still hear the squealing pitch of her voice, teasing me about the dullness of my scales, my skinny arms, and the way I wore my hair down and wild. At eleven, all I'd ever wanted to do was explore with Havamal. I wasn't like the other girls I knew. Most of the time, I didn't care how I looked when there were exciting things to do. But still, the screech of Vigdis's laughter and the way the other girls spat out more insults in agreement had sent me fleeing from the glacier to the safety of one of our secret wrecks.

When I'd reached the ancient ship, I went straight for the captain's abandoned cabin. Slamming the door behind me, I sank to the moldering floor. Grateful for the privacy the open archways of the glacier didn't provide, I braced my back against the door. I don't know how long I cried there, bringing my fists up to my mouth to stifle the noise, before I heard someone flop down on the other side of the door.

I never wondered who it was. I knew it was Havamal by the way he stayed silent, just being there with me as my friend while

I sobbed out my misery. Finally, when I choked back the last of my tears, he pushed against the door. I scooted along the rotting floor to make a space for him to come inside.

He approached me like a scared animal, moving slowly with one hand raised. Then he lowered himself to the floor beside me and wrapped his scrawny arm around my shoulders. At the time, his small arm felt impossibly strong and unendingly reliable. I laid my head on his chest and let the steady rise and fall of his breathing comfort me. He brought a little of his inner heat to the surface of his scales, warming me gently, even though he didn't have any spare fat and doing it must have cost him.

"It doesn't matter," he whispered into the dim light. "What they say doesn't matter."

"Why? Because they're stupid?" I joked, pawing at my eyes. "It's not just them. All the adults think it, too. I've heard what some of them say to Mama."

"But I don't think it," he said, and flashed me that gap-toothed smile I loved so much. At the time, his words were the only thing that mattered. "And we're going to escape, right? Just you and me. So let them say what they want."

I nuzzled under his chin while he held me. Together, we stayed like that until we fell asleep, leaving only after morning came.

Now I leaned my head back against the ice wall in the dungeon. These memories sometimes seemed like a dream, now—or a nightmare, given the amount of bittersweet pain they brought with them. Even if Havamal apologized every day until our dying breaths, there was no going back to the way things had been. Back then my trust in him had been absolute. When we were kids, I couldn't see anything in him but the good.

I wondered what the boy Havamal had been would think of me now. He'd always seen the best in me, too. How would he have reacted, knowing what I'd done to Vigdis? Knowing what a selfish person I'd become? I could almost look into the young, hopeful face of his past and see the disappointment flickering in his bright eyes.

SOMETIME LATER, I HEARD SCUFFLING outside the door. I moved toward it, half hoping that Havamal had come back. The ice boulder was shoved aside and, before my eyes could adjust to the new light, a pair of rough hands grabbed me by my arms. A harpoon pressed into my back.

"Get moving," a voice hissed in my ear. I recognized it as the king's enforcer, the bailiff who handed out judgments and punishments. Leif was a merman the size of an orca calf, with a neck so thick it blended into his jaw. His fins were blood red. We all knew and feared his voice.

Even though Havamal had said they wouldn't mark me, I swallowed hard. "Where… where are we going?" I stammered. "Is it the trial already?"

"The king and I just want to ask you a few questions."

If I'd had anything left in my stomach, I would have thrown up. I let the guard drag me along the hallway as the bailiff swam behind us with his weapon raised. I couldn't help thinking that Havamal was wrong and they were going to torture me anyway.

He ushered me into the main hall. It was empty except for the king, perched on his throne with his midnight-blue tail tucked behind him. His dark eyes fixed on me, unblinking. The absence of his guards made me more nervous. What were they going to do to me that they didn't want anyone else to see?

"I am going to keep this brief," the king said, steepling his fingers and sitting back on his throne. "Tell the physicians how to fix Vigdis, and I may be more lenient with you at your sentencing."

I took a deep steadying breath. Maybe I wasn't here to be tortured? It surprised me that Calder cared about Vigdis. I didn't know what had happened, much less how to help her.

"My guard said she was pregnant?" I said cautiously.

The king sat forward on his throne, an incredulous scowl forming on his face. "She has a monster growing inside her."

It was the worst outcome I could imagine, and Loki had made it true.

"There isn't a way," I whispered. "I made the bargain with a god…"

"You made a bargain with a god to hurt a fellow mermaid?" The king tilted forward and stared at me. "Everyone is talking about it. And it makes me look bad if I can't even get to the bottom of what happened."

So it was about his appearance, not Vigdis, after all.

"No, for a mate, for her." My voice was so tiny. I couldn't look at him.

"You expect me to believe that all of this was for her benefit?"

Close to tears, I shook my head.

The king made a noise of disgust, then motioned to his bailiff. "Take her back to her cell. I'll get the real answers out of Havamal."

*   *   *

AT THE TRIAL, VIGDIS STOOD in the corner, apart from the rest of the court. Her belly bulged, covered in a network of blue-violet veins, though she'd been carrying only a week. The doctor testified that there was no egg, even though the shapeshifter had appeared in his merform while he seduced her. Her pregnancy was almost mammalian, with the creature connected directly to her womb and wrapped in a sack of tissue. Its veins had woven too tightly alongside hers—to cut it out might kill her, the midwives said.

The rest of her body had grown skeletal as the animal inside her stole her nutrients. Based on the way she looked, leaving it inside her womb might kill her too.

As I stood on the dais in front of the king, guilt threatened to strangle me. I'd done this to her. My selfishness might kill her. Even if I never expected this, I'd cajoled her into giving up her voice. She couldn't even tell the court what had happened.

The guards had apprehended the "father" of the parasite growing inside her: a creature the king classified as a sea-swine, a shifter governed by the god of mischief. When they dragged me from the cells, I saw the creature at a distance. Its front half looked like a land animal, with cloven hooves and a hooked smile framed by sharp, ivory tusks. Its body tapered into the tail of an orca. But the most horrifying features of the creature were the unblinking eyes that covered its entire hide, letting it see from all angles, just as Vigdis's mother had said.

The king had ordered his personal guards to watch the creature at all times. They had locked it in a deeper cell than mine. It was not subject to our laws, so they couldn't put it on trial. And no one dared to kill a creature sent by the gods—even a creature like that, even one sent by a god like Loki.

Vigdis, silent, kept her eyes on the floor. Everyone else murmured around us.

I trembled on the stand. I'd been waiting for an hour for my chance to speak, but now that the opportunity had come, the words died. I wanted to tell the court that I didn't have a choice. I wanted to scream that it wasn't my fault, that Loki had twisted my words around and made a mockery of a bargain that should have brought all of us happiness. Vigdis's fuchsia eyes bore into me, accusing and angry. The rage inside her seemed to beat against the prison of her silence.

My shaking fingers gripped the edges of the witness stand. I struggled to hover in one place. My new legs constantly reached out for things to grasp and climb. So the bailiff had improvised. He dragged a heavy anchor from one of the capsized ships into the court. Then he wrapped the chain around my waist, circled the stand with it to bind me to the ice, and left the anchor near the king's throne. I couldn't imagine how I must look: a monster whose legs thrashed against the bonds, reaching for members of the assembled crowd, even while tears ran down her face. Merfolk waiting with bated breath filled all the rows in the court amphitheater. Before, I'd been more or less invisible. Now I was a spectacle.

I took a deep breath. "I never meant for it to happen like this. I just didn't want to do it… I didn't want to pick a mate."

The bailiff swam closer, clutching a tablet of ice against his chest. "Can you be more specific?" he asked. "The whole glacier wants to hear—the king needs to hear—the whole thing in your own words."

When I looked at the rows of people, I expected to see nothing but fear and hatred. Instead, I watched as an old neighbor draped her arms over Mama's shoulder, and a former teacher of mine made eye contact with me and gave me a sad smile. A few looked angry. Most of them were sitting near a slender merwoman with coral hair like Vigdis's. My breath shortened as panic and guilt fought to erupt. But everyone else... everyone else just looked haunted, pitying. They felt sorry for me. I swallowed. I hadn't expected them to feel sorry for me. Maybe I hadn't been as alone in the glacier as I'd always imagined.

The king gave his deputy a pointed look, and the bailiff cleared his throat. "Ersel?"

"I made a deal," I whispered, looking down. Suddenly, I couldn't say anything else. "I'm so sorry."

The king banged his whalebone staff on the ice. His advisers, hovering on his left side, exchanged glances. "By your own confession, you've been found guilty as an accessory to this attack."

"She's a victim too!' I heard Mama shout from somewhere in the crowd. Of course she would defend me to the end. Part of me wanted to smile, but I couldn't. "She's just a child..."

I closed my eyes. I expected sadness and loss to wash over me, but after a week starving in the dark, alone with my guilt, I was too numb.

The king gestured to my legs, and I thought I saw a smile ghost across his lips. Of course he would take pleasure in exiling and punishing someone who dared to want something other than his system. "Although I can see that your decision and your deal with the trickster have also resulted in punishment of you by imprisoning you in this form, the magnitude of your actions against Vigdis and the fact that they may still claim her life have left us no option. Our laws are clear about attempted murder. You are banished from the glacier and will lose five scales from your back. If you return, all your scales will be pulled from your body, and you will be left to starve on the ice shelf."

One of the advisors whispered into the king's ear, and the monarch shook his head in disgust. "Did you really do all this for a human?"

Havamal had told him about Ragna, then. I should have felt more fear, but after the sentence he'd just pronounced, how much worse could it get?

Still, I had to clear my throat three times before I forced the words through chattering teeth. "No, Your Majesty. I did it for myself."

I respected Ragna. I admired her wildness and her fierce independence, even as they made me envious. Yes, part of me wished I could have had time to see what could grow between us, but when it came down to it, my choices had been for me.

I looked at Havamal, who was hovering behind the king's throne. He didn't meet my gaze, but his eyes were bloodshot and rimmed in black. He looked broken. When I looked more closely, I noticed an inflamed and swollen patch of exposed red skin running across his torso where a row of scales should have been. Catching my look, he covered his stomach with his arms and gave a tiny shrug. He'd said that the king wouldn't mark *me* before the trial. He'd only hinted at his own fate.

At King Calder's direction, two bailiffs swam forward armed with bone staffs. They each seized one of my arms and spread me out like a starfish. I heard someone else screaming. The extractor approached next and brandished his shark-tooth blade.

WHEN THE ORDEAL WAS OVER, the bailiff dragged me, still crying, to the edge of the glacier. King Calder and the rest of our community followed in his shadow, waiting to see him push the monster from the ledge and into the endless deep. We always finished trials at night, so the water outside the glacier was black.

Without giving me time to say goodbye to anyone, the bailiff marched me down the long outcropping of ice that made up our main underwater entrance. I didn't look behind me, but I could hear people shuffling and scraping, trying to get closer. I was sure that some of them just wanted a last look at the freak—a memory to keep for their children about what happened when you went against the king.

The bailiff jabbed his harpoon into the small of my back. The blade nicked my skin and I yelped. The merman just laughed. He probably thought an extra cut served me right.

At the edge of the platform, I raised my eyes and murmured a last prayer to Odin before I dove into the watery loneliness that awaited me.

I drifted until I touched the ocean bottom. My new legs were clumsy and hard to maneuver, but at least the seabed gave me something to follow. I made my nest inside the hull of an abandoned ship with the skeletons of the dead for company. Barnacles had claimed most of the interior, and forests of seaweed grew through the cracked floor, but the cabin at the rear remained mostly intact. It wasn't a welcoming home, but I needed a place to hide out of the open water. Without my tail and my fins, I was slow and vulnerable. Anything could catch me as I lumbered through the water. And I doubted even the belugas would accept me as their friend now.

When I wrenched the cabin door open, a whole human life seemed to surround me: a body, a room full of trinkets, animal skins bloated with water, a table laid for a last meal with an empty plate and perfectly aligned cutlery. I threw the pieces of the skeleton outside, into his watery grave, and claimed his space for my own.

The king had allowed me to take a small bundle with me. No food. No kelp. Nothing to help me survive outside the glacier on my own. I was allowed sentimental things; I'd taken my human trinkets. Ragna's necklace dangled around my throat, and a comb of my mother's pearls adorned my hair. It was ironic, how well-groomed and adorned I looked now, when no one was here to see me.

I tried to rest on the watery bed, to clear my head of memories and the pain of my missing scales. But my new legs had other ideas. As I laid my head back, they explored: touching, sucking, grasping everything in the cabin. The noise they made and the constant sensation of uncontrolled movement kept me awake. A human sword leaned against the bedframe. I grabbed it, held it to my breast, and pondered driving it into my heart. Then I positioned it over one of the tentacles, imagining what it would be like to hack them off, one by one. But I didn't have the courage, and some hope remained. Maybe I could make this right. Maybe there was still something I could do.

Until then, I'd never sleep.

Part 2: Princess of Ice

The old poets sing of Love and Honesty
as sisters standing arm in arm.
But Love has two sisters and her arm locks
also in Deception's cold embrace.

ICE TABLET C76

"In the midst of this spot stood a house,
built with the bones of shipwrecked human beings.
There sat the sea witch, allowing a toad to eat from
her mouth, just as people sometimes feed
a canary with a piece of sugar."

—Hans Christian Andersen, *The Little Mermaid*

One

HOURS LATER, A FAINT GREEN light pulsed under the door. I wanted to curl up into a tight ball and ignore it. I wanted to pretend I was hallucinating, but one of the tentacles reached out and grasped the cabin's door handle, pulling it open.

Loki swam in. They were wearing their signature horned helmet, but their body had transformed into the form of a human woman. Blonde hair floated around their shoulders, and a white top clung to their slender, muscular form. Dark brown eyes flecked with gold stared at me, rich and deep. If not for the helmet and the cruelty in their beautiful smile, I wouldn't have recognized them.

I wished I could control my new legs well enough to strangle Loki. I didn't know if it was possible to strangle a god, but I longed to try. My tentacles flailed uselessly, and Loki laughed.

"You lied to me," I spat.

"Now, now, little Ersel," they chided, removing their helmet and placing it on the rotting table. The voice that passed through their lips was female: high, patronizing, and instantly grating. It was a voice I recognized immediately as the one that had belonged to Vigdis. "I never lied. You just weren't very specific about the things you wanted."

"Right. You've been watching me, you chose me, you offered me legs, and you thought I wanted these?" I sat up and glared at them, focusing all my energy on their left cheek. A tentacle splayed forth and clapped them across the side of the head—not hard, but a victory of control nonetheless.

Loki stumbled backward; their mocking grin slipped.

"And Vigdis?" I demanded. "You sent that creature to her. She wanted a mate. She wanted children to love. She gave you her voice in exchange. You knew what she wanted, and instead you gave her a monster."

"She liked him well enough at first." Loki rubbed the back of their head. "I gave you what you asked for. Learn to be more specific."

My mouth gaped, opening and closing like a salmon. "Learn? I learned never to trust you again. I learned that I can't have what I want because it gets other people hurt. Get out and leave me alone."

They threw up their hands and spun around the room. "Shall I leave you to all of this? Have you decided to make this your palace?"

"What choice do I have?"

Their eyes gleamed with green light. "There's always a choice. Let me make you another proposition. I just wanted to up the stakes a little, before... make it all seem more worth your while. Maybe now you'll have learned to be more specific about what you ask for. Go on."

I crossed my arms over my chest. "No."

"I'm your only way out of this. You're banished. You can't even see your mother again. You're a cursed animal, living in a ship full of human bones. You can change that, but I'm the only one who can help you." Loki caught one of my tentacles when I tried to hit them again and stroked the slimy topside. "Do you want to be *this* forever?"

Their words made my stomach clench. I hated them for what they'd done to me and to Vigdis. I hated myself for letting it happen. But they weren't lying. No one else could help me fix this. They were my tormenter and my salvation. Worse, they knew it.

"What is the deal?" I asked.

A sly smile came over their face. "Three voices this time. One human, one beast, one mer."

"One beast? How am I supposed to convince an animal to give me its voice? I can't take it by force... I won't. They have to agree, don't they? For the magic to work?"

Loki snapped their fingers. "That's your problem. You have to bring me three voices, and those are the types I need. You can grant them anything in return."

"For what? Why do you need them all? Surely you must have thousands in your collection by now, enough to match your limitless forms."

They shrugged, eyes narrowing. "You don't need to know my reasons. Do we have a deal or don't we?"

My mind traveled back to Ragna and the last day we spent together. Was all this worth it? Just to escape? To have the land to explore? I'd only known Ragna for a short time, but I'd learned that her life was nowhere close to perfect.

I imagined her pursing her lips and rowing toward the open ocean until her muscles cramped. She would paddle to her revenge with all the strength she had. She'd make it; the lust for freedom would push her little boat as if a team of whales dragged her through the sea. I wanted that freedom, and I wanted my revenge, but was making another deal with this monster worth it?

I sighed and pressed a kiss to the pendant at my throat.

"Before I bring you the third voice, you must give me what I want. Any tricks, any lies, anything less than what I desire, and the whole deal is off. The voices return to their owners."

Loki raised an eyebrow. "See, you're learning after all."

The sincerity in their gaze told me they believed it, but I wasn't sure I agreed with them. As they vanished in a green cyclone, I prayed to Odin to give me the wisdom to beat the trickster at their own game.

*   *   *

MY TRAP WAS EMPTY. FOR the third day in a row, the stick remained in place and the square basket I'd woven to net crabs stayed braced and ready. I exhaled slowly, trying to ignore the gnawing hunger tearing at me.

Since leaving the glacier a week before, I'd managed to catch only a single crab by myself. By the time I removed the creature's shell, there wasn't much meat left. I'd devoured it so quickly that I couldn't remember how it tasted.

I couldn't find the materials to fashion my own harpoon, and I'd never been trained with one. If I still had my fins, I would be able to swim fast enough to catch smaller fish without need of weapons or traps. As it was, I couldn't catch a floating seagull. I had no desire to eat one of the birds, but in my desperation, even the stringy land-meat sounded appetizing.

On the third day, I'd made the crawl to the belugas' surfacing pod for sun. The matriarch had recognized me and welcomed me. She'd spared my new legs no more than a glance before butting her head against the side of my hip. I'd never been more grateful for a kind touch. The whales had fed me that day, brought me a still-flopping grayling and tossed it onto the ice. But food was getting harder and harder to find as more human fishing parties came north, and I didn't want to deprive the pod too often.

The missing scales on my back made movement agonizing. Although the wound had closed and scabbed quickly, the area tightened every time I lifted my arms, and the freezing ocean water stung the exposed skin. Sighing with disappointment and pain, I walked along the sand, back to my den in the ship's cabin. After bashing the door open with a sideways kick of my tentacles, I wandered in and settled onto my wooden frame bed.

I'd given myself a week to tend to my physical and emotional wounds, but now I needed to make progress on the deal I'd made with the trickster.

I couldn't force an animal to give me its voice, and in order to negotiate I had to be able to communicate. My mind wandered back to the belugas Ragna had trained to sing on command and to the whale with the terrible voice. She had been so proud of her training, and the whale hadn't known or cared that his voice made me want to cover my ears. I might be able to communicate well enough with the belugas to make them understand what I wanted, but I couldn't deprive the gentle creatures of even a part of their happiness, not when they accepted and fed me after my own kind had cast me out.

There was an orca pod in the area that might understand my gesturing and inquiries, but somehow I couldn't bring myself to seek it out. On one hand, I feared what the ocean killers could do to me now that I was in another form and clearly marked as an exile. Their respect for the merfolk was tenuous and subject to constant negotiation. On the other hand, I didn't want to see an orca miserable, either.

Of all the creatures I knew, there was only one beast I knew that spoke the *godstongue.*

But to speak to Loki's creature, I had to risk everything. The idea was insane, and yet, once it took hold, I knew I had to act before fear dissuaded me. I shot out of the bed and winced as my quick movement jarred the wound.

I crawled along the seabed, as close to the underside of the glacier as I dared, creeping along in the silt. I was so deep in the water, I doubted I'd be noticed. Crabs scuttled along the sand and over my tentacles. They clicked their claws as they scooped up fragments of fish carcass that had sunk from above.

Sunlight barely reached the bottom, but looking up, I could see the silver-blue reflection of the glacier. The pools of dark shadow running along the ice told me that it was sundown, or near to it. I hoped that most of the merfolk would be tucked into their ice caves, settling in to sleep after dinner.

The strip of exposed, raw skin where my scales had been throbbed. The extractor knew his work. He'd flayed a palm-sized area of my back so quickly I couldn't register the excruciating pain until after he was finished. I imagined what it would be like to lie completely scaleless and bleeding on the ice while the sun pelted down on my blistered flesh and shuddered. I couldn't afford to get caught.

Pushing off with my legs, I propelled myself upward. Swimming with the tentacles instead of my normal fins was exhausting. In order to move, my whole body had to contract and shut like a trap. I tried to control my breathing. All merfolk make a suctioning noise to draw air into our gills while moving, but I didn't want any noise to alert the guards.

At the slick, smooth base of the ice mountain, my tentacles acted of their own accord. I flipped over and blood rushed to my head as water flowed up my nostrils. But my legs anchored me to the ice; suction prevented me from slipping or being carried too far by the water's pull. For the first time, I wondered if Loki had accidentally given me a secret weapon.

But how would I climb inside without being seen, especially when full control of my limbs still evaded me? I focused all my thoughts and energy on the slim crevice that ran along the underside of the ice mountain and into the central hall. It was too narrow for whales or sharks. Anything else that might venture in could pose no harm.

The tentacles raced toward it, running along the ice, operated by some primal, fishlike part of my brain. A lone guard waited outside the crevice. My limbs reached for him before I could think and twisted his fragile body in a powerful grip. I tried to release him, but I couldn't. My heart pounded, and primal instinct overrode my control.

The merman tried to scream, but as soon as he opened his mouth, one of my tentacles plunged down his throat. I felt him go limp, and fought to let him go with all my strength. His heart kept beating even though he had lost consciousness. Loki had truly made me into a monster, but I could avoid becoming a killer.

I focused on the crevice. My tentacles released their victim and scuttled through the opening into the heart of the ice fortress. My limbs braced against both sides of the walls, and I climbed quickly up the long tunnel. As I climbed, the familiar hum of voices echoed through the walls. I wondered what Mama was doing. Was she still going to meals after my disgrace? Or was she huddling in our ice cave with her dinner, truly alone now that I was gone?

The hall was dark, but I'd grown up here and I knew the inside of the fortress like the back of my hand, by smell as well as sight. Scuttling down the hall, I made my way to the very center of the ice mountain—to the dungeons, where they'd secured Loki's demon.

My scales quivered. The king might have stationed ten guards or more around the prisoner. My new legs were strong, but I didn't know how many I could fight. And with ten guards all trying to grab me at once, how much control would I have? Would I kill one?

Using the sticky cups on the bottoms of the tentacles, I walked along the ceiling. It was so cold at the heart of the glacier that the ice burned my slippery new flesh. Deep cold ran through my body. I hadn't been to the surface in days. I wondered how skinny I looked and longed for the warmth of my scales after soaking in the sun.

Positioned on either side of the cell entrance, two guards muttered to each other. One of them had silver scales and bronze muscles. The sight of him made my stomach hurt with something that was neither hate nor love. Faced with the opportunity to hurt him, I didn't feel any desire for revenge. I bit my tongue to stifle a cry. Even after what Havamal had done, some part of me still wanted both of us to be happy. And he had suffered, too. I'd seen the band of missing scales around his waist at my trial. But when I peered at the guards and studied their faces, I realized the silver-finned merman wasn't Havamal at all.

I scuttled into position above them, then dropped from the ceiling with my tentacles spread out into a fan like a manta ray. I focused on my goal: getting past these mermen to the prison cavern. My body took over. My legs whipped sideways, out of my control and yet beautiful in their deadly precision. One of the guards screamed, but a stray tentacle knocked him sideways and his voice quietened. He slumped against the ice wall, but his chest continued to rise and fall. The other guard's eyes widened, and he swam past me, racing for the exit and the safety of the central hall. I cursed. I couldn't catch up with him.

With most of the glacier on the verge of sleep, it would take the merman a few minutes to gather more guards. Still, I didn't have much time.

The king's men had secured the cell with a grate from the inside of a sunken ship; even King Calder realized the potential in human inventions when circumstances required improvisation. The grate was partially frozen into the glacier and would take at least four men to move. Our law didn't have provisions for holding criminals below after their trials. Had the monster been one of the merfolk, his scales would have been stripped and he'd have been left to die on the ice shelf.

I swallowed hard, and clutched the new vial that hung around my neck. I would meet that fate if they caught me. But maybe I'd deserve it. After all, the only thing I could imagine the monster asking for was freedom, and if I provided that, any new crimes he committed would be my fault.

But it seemed a crueler fate than death to leave him imprisoned indefinitely. Did Loki's creatures die? Would the shapeshifter remain here throughout the generations, never fading, never able to leave?

My tentacles wrapped around the heavy grate's iron bars and lifted it as easily as a basket of kelp. The fallen guard moaned, but then stilled. I tossed the bars to the side. From deep inside the cavern, the sea-swine rose and peered over the edge of the crevice into the labyrinth of ice. His torso reminded me of the land creatures called boars that were depicted in some sculptures. At the center of each scale, he had an unblinking eye. His body tapered into a twisted, black tail with pointed fins.

When the animal saw me, he hesitated. All of his red-rimmed eyes burned into me. I gulped. The greatest danger might not be meeting my end atop the ice shelf, but being gored by the foot-long tusks that stuck out from the sea-swine's snout.

I braced myself, spreading my tentacles wider to make my body look as large and dangerous as possible, the way some fish did when we hunted them. Looking into dozens of unblinking irises on the creature's hide made me more aware of the vulnerability of my own single pair of eyes, and I turned my face to the side to protect them.

The creature folded its tail under its massive body and crouched on the ice. Then he said the last thing I expected. "I'm not supposed to leave."

"What?" I brandished Loki's vial at him. "I'm here to make a deal."

His ears perked up, and his snout quivered. Then all his eyes focused on the glass bottle in my hand. "Loki actually sent you to me? At last? They're ready to forgive me?"

Forgiveness? We only had minutes before the guard would return with reinforcements. Everything about his behavior confused me. But as Loki's creature, the monster probably had some insight into how the god thought, and I needed all the information I could get. I folded my tentacles and sat beside him. "Loki didn't send me, but they gave me this task. I need to find three voices. One of them has to come from a beast."

He sighed. "Well, a beast I am, but they'll never accept a voice from me."

I folded my arms across my chest. "They never gave me any restrictions. They didn't say I couldn't use your voice." I locked my smile behind my teeth. If Loki wouldn't want the sea-swine's voice, I had even more motivation to make this deal. "Loki is the god of wordplay, of precision. They're going to have to accept the terms they offered."

A gleeful feeling warmed my chest. I'd found a technicality Loki hadn't thought of. If the sea-swine's voice wasn't what he wanted, that was too bad.

"There's only one thing I want, and Loki won't ever allow it." All of the pig's thousand eyes shut at once. I jumped; I had not realized the bulging eyes had lids. His long tongued flicked out as he spoke. It was almost impossible to imagine this creature as the dashing merman Vigdis's mother had described. "They put me into this form a long time ago. It's better for everyone that I stay imprisoned. I'm safe enough until there is a storm."

I remembered the thunder that had rumbled through the glacier the night Vigdis's wish came true.

The swine shuddered. "When there is a storm… I can't control my mind. I become Loki's plaything. No one is safe near me then. The worst is that during storms I become beautiful … and it's all too easy for me to act out Loki's viciousness when it's concealed behind a smile."

"What happens during storms? What were you… before?" I braced myself, almost dreading the answer.

"I was a human," the swine said. "I fought for Loki in a war before your time, but then I turned on them to fight for Thor. The trickster captured me during one of the battles. Loki… they don't forgive those who betray them. I was too insignificant for Thor to risk everything and save me, not when the war was over and they all wanted to forget and make peace."

My heart pounded faster. In order to gain my freedom, I would have to get the better of Loki. But what would they do to me if I tried and failed? They had already turned me into a monster, but I still had my free will. At least, I thought I did.

The creature's voice dropped almost to a whisper. "When storms come, they remind me of my treachery. The storms are Thor's blessing, and Loki uses them to undo me. When they come, my mind becomes Loki's. I do only their bidding."

"When you seduced Vigdis… you had no control?"

He shrugged. "Not very much."

"Do you even realize what you're doing?"

"Yes. It's like my mind is trapped and I watch my actions through someone else's gaze. My body moves but I'm powerless... just a passenger in my own skin. But as I said," he hesitated, then licked his crusty lips. My stomach churned. "At the time I enjoy it, so perhaps I do not resist Loki as much as I should. And I don't know what that says about me. Your friend was very beautiful. Romancing her ... it was not the worst task the trickster has given me."

The full weight of that horror bore down on me. I could sympathize because of the limited control I had over my tentacles. But what would it be like to commit atrocities as this creature had, to know it was your body that acted, but have no ability to stop? If I angered Loki further... if I lost to him... that fate could become mine.

I looked at the swine, and my sick feeling intensified. But if Loki made me do evil things, curse or no curse, I would at least try to resist them, even if they somehow outsmarted me again, and I lost whatever shadow of freedom I still had. No matter how long I remained chained to them, I promised myself I would always try to fight against enjoying the twisted fantasies they enacted through me or comforting myself with my own powerlessness. Perhaps this creature deserved to lose his voice because, trickster god or not, he was responsible, too.

"What is it that you want?" I asked. "To be human again?"

"Nothing so complicated as that." The swine studied his hooves. "I want to die. I've been alive for more than a millennium and all but thirty years in this cursed form. I can't kill myself. I've tried."

I tugged the vial from my neck so violently the rope snapped. My fingers trembled around the little bottle. *Anything*, Loki had said. No caveats. For a moment, I wondered if they had expected me to choose this course all along. But I didn't believe they were capable of mercy, not after what the sea-swine had told me—a millennium. I started to pull the cork, shaking so badly I nearly dropped the bottle.

Was I about to become a killer? Would I be a murderer, or a dispenser of long-overdue justice?

The sea-swine leaned forward and nudged my hand with his snout.

I teased the cork fully out. A white liquid flowed up from the creature's throat like silvery bile. His voice filled the vial to the brim. I had to be careful not to let even a drop spill as I sealed the container.

A smile of triumph appeared on the swine's face. Slowly, his form shifted. The unblinking eyes vanished, and then his massive tail split in two. As his body transformed into that of a human male, the creature began choking on the freezing water. My eyes snapped to his neck, the smooth plane of skin where his gills had been.

The swine laughed while he drowned. Thunder cracked overhead, and I imagined that Thor was laughing too. I didn't wait for him to die. I grabbed the vial by its chain, unwilling to hang it from my neck; I didn't want the creature's polluted voice hovering so close to my heart. Then, pushing off the glacier's wall with all the strength in my legs, I swam away as the creature's life bled into the ocean.

Two

WHEN LOKI RETURNED TO COLLECT the sea-swine's voice, they didn't speak a word. They arrived with no visual illusions—in a slender androgynous body, lips bound together with a thousand painful threads. Their scars were a reminder that all the gods were cruel, and that even Loki had known pain. But it wasn't an excuse for what they had become, and none of us knew the original sin that had provoked Odin's ire. Anger heated the ocean around them as they entered my tiny shipman's cabin. Wordless, they snatched the new vial from the table and left, slamming the door so hard behind them that one of the rusted hinges flew off.

Their fury was enough to give me a surge of happiness that allowed me to sleep through the night for the first time since my transformation. Loki had never believed that I might be brave or stupid enough to return to the glacier, or that I would seek out the dangerous creature who had seduced Vigdis.

Well, I was through doing what the trickster expected.

But our bargain had been made more than a month ago, and I'd started to lose hope of completing their task. I couldn't bring myself to think about stealing another mermaid's voice. I knew I must, but I wanted that sin to have purpose. If I couldn't obtain a human voice, I couldn't complete the deal with Loki. And to find a human, I'd just have to wait.

A few ships had passed through the ice trap unscathed as the calm weather lured the humans' tribes north to hunt whales and seals along the fracturing ice shelf. But the humans never docked, never stopped long enough in the icy waters to make camp or venture onto the precarious ice shelf. Most of them knew better, and, thanks to Ragna's explanation, I knew why. It simply wasn't worth the risk.

Today, I waited at the edge of the belugas' abandoned surfacing hole. Our weather was finally starting to warm up, though this far north, we would always have ice. When summer began, the whales no longer worried about finding a place to breathe and dispersed throughout the sea to hunt. The warming water kept the hole in the ice open, and it widened each day. I had fashioned a sort of spear from a slender strip of wood that I found in one of the ship's hulls. The belugas took me with them when they hunted, patiently accepted my ineffective spear thrusts, and kept me fed. Part of me hoped that Ragna would come back and seek me out now that the water was a little less treacherous, while at other times I hoped she was halfway across the world making a new life for herself.

I shut my eyes against the warming sun. I knew by now that the gods wouldn't dissolve my pact with Loki, though I prayed to Odin every night to change me back. I wanted the All-Father to rewind time, to make it so Vigdis was never attacked, so that

I never met Ragna. If I hadn't known her, I couldn't miss her so much now.

Red sails appeared on the horizon, and a moment later a dark ship began winding its way through the channels in the melting ice shelf. The bow was adorned with the outline of a skinny mermaid holding a shell. I snorted. I'd seen the design on more than one passing titan. It was ironic that most humans didn't believe in us, yet featured us so proudly on their ships.

The hull sat low in the water; the ocean crept up the ship's sides, reaching almost to the deck. Whatever the ship carried, it was heavy. As it drew alongside me, I ducked under the water. Sailors dressed in rich furs leaned over the rail, searching the sea. They clutched long metal spears and shouted to one another over the loud splashing of the oars. I scanned the men one by one, hoping beyond reason that I might catch a flash of sun-blonde hair or a glimpse of a fierce girl in an oversized fur coat. I couldn't even be sure if I missed her or just having someone—anyone—to talk to.

Cutting through the water, a black-finned orca sped past me. She had a notch the shape of a half-moon on her dorsal fin, and I recognized her as the matriarch of one of the local pods—a group the merfolk of my clan often hunted alongside. A moment later, the whole sea seemed full of orcas; a legion of black fins streaked above the surface of the water like toy boats with midnight sails.

Ducking under the waves, I listened to them speak. Although I couldn't understand their words, everyone knew that the orcas spoke a sophisticated language. I could have studied the whales' tongues, but master linguists were becoming rarer and rarer in the ice mountain, and I doubted one of them would have agreed to take me as an apprentice. The orcas' language was considered one of the most difficult whale languages for merfolk to master. The first female gave directions; her voice was high and ethereal. The water carried her words to the rest of the pod.

The group split in two. The females with calves at their sides went one way, staying deep under the ocean, while the rest of the pod went another. I could see what they were trying to do, and it pulled at my heartstrings. The orcas knew that ship carried men who had come to kill them. They were trying to save their babies.

On the ship's deck, the sailors' shouting turned to curses. But they didn't fall for the whales' trick. Clipping the ice and sending glassy shards flying in its wake, the great boat pursued the calves. My heart sank. Against this many humans, I didn't know how to help the whales. I shuddered. Maybe the reason the ship sat so low in the water was that it was already overburdened with the bodies of whales the men had killed. With a ship that size, the length of a sperm whale at least, they could take a dozen orca calves.

The whales' chattering became more frenzied. I could sense their fear in the vibrations that carried through the waves. The pod dodged in and out of the icebergs, leading the ship into the frozen heart of our deathtrap.

My whole body tensed. The humans on the ship's deck were whooping and shouting, wild with bloodlust and the thrill of the chase. I sensed disaster pending. If one of the humans pierced a whale with a spear, I could remove it—if the orcas still recognized me as a friend.

The ship chased the whale pod, trying to herd them away from the treacherous bergs. When it passed less than an arm's length from me, I pushed off the ice and attached myself to its hull. I still hadn't mastered the art of swimming without my fins, but I'd come to appreciate some things about the tentacles. The ship towed me like an oversized barnacle. I dangled upside-down and watched the whales maneuver.

Above me, one of the men projected his voice above the deck's chaos. "Milord, we can't follow them through there again. The ship's too wide. The ice hasn't melted enough. We'll crash on a berg."

The rowers hesitated, and the ship drifted to the left, pulled by the tide toward the shelf. I heard a cracking noise above me. The oars twisted and churned with renewed vigor.

"One of those calves will feed my family for the whole winter," another male voice roared. "The ice here is receding. It'll be soft and break easy." One of the oars clipped the edge of the shelf and a slab of ice—as long and sharp as a blade—fractured into the sea. "See, the ice is no problem. It'll crumble if we hit it."

The ship jolted, and I almost lost my grip. The momentary hesitation cost the humans. From my underwater vantage point, I could see the whales' silhouettes fading into the ocean's blue haze.

"We're losing them!" The leader yelled. Feet scuffled across the deck, and I heard the cracking noise again, followed by a shriek of pain. We coasted forward, gliding through the sea like a shadowy kraken.

Suddenly, the ship lurched much more forcefully, and screams and shouts sounded from the deck: "What was that?"

"What did we hit?"

"Captain?"

"There's water coming through…"

"Turn around, go back to the shelf!"

I could hear them racing around the deck like seabirds. Then metal and wood groaned, and the ship reversed course. The whales' chatter quietened to a low hum. I remembered Mama telling me once that with orcas, silence meant danger. A long time ago, our glacier community had gone to war against the orcas. Our histories still told the bloody stories, and it had never happened again. Both sides had lost too many to think that victory was worth the deaths.

I released my grip on the hull and floated to the nearest iceberg. Splintered wood stuck out from the ice where the ship stabbed into the berg like a human spear in the side of a giant beluga. But it was the ship that was dying. Pushing my hair back from my eyes, I watched the men try to row as the ship sank lower in the water. I should have felt relief that my opportunity to obtain a human voice had come, but I felt only sickness spreading from my stomach up to my throat and making me dizzy.

The humans were screaming and praying to Aegir to save them. But everyone knew the whales were the sea god's favorite children. The orcas swam nearer, clustering silently around their iceberg savior, waiting for the humans to fall into their domain.

The men broke off pieces of the sinking ship. A few roped together makeshift rafts and drifted into the water. Others climbed to the top of the mast or dangled from the ropes that suspended the sails. The orcas chattered, ducking their heads together like old mermen hunching over a gaming board. I bit my lip. I didn't have to understand their language to know what they were planning.

With a cry, one of the men fell from the mast. He was a large-framed fellow, with shoulder-length golden hair and green boots that looked as if they were woven from fish scales. His gold curls reminded me of Ragna. Before the orcas could close in, I pushed off from the ice and swam to him. Snatching him under the armpits, I dragged him toward the ice shelf. He tried to scream, swallowed cold water, and sent a flurry of bubbles to the surface. One of the orcas trilled at me reproachfully. The man kicked at my sides, trying to free himself, but I held fast. He could be the only opportunity I would get.

We surfaced as the water around us turned pink. Tendrils of red snaked into the sea, and color exploded in the artic grayness. The man in my grasp stilled, and I thought I could hear him moaning over the screams, the splashes, and the crunch of bones.

Although it was summer, the water was only a few degrees warmer than the ice. I shivered, but forced warmth up through my scales. I needed to keep this man warm enough to survive. Any of the others the orcas didn't slaughter would freeze to death or drown.

Using my tentacles, I lifted the sailor onto the edge of the ice. He scooted away from the edge and shook as the frigid air bit into his wet body. Rubbing the salt water from his eyes, he looked over my head at the scene, the one-sided battle between the whales and their victims. I'd already seen enough.

Bracing himself on his hands, the sailor vomited into the sea. Then he brought a shaking hand up to cover his mouth.

"I don't mean to harm you," I said.

"Are you from Aegir?" he whispered, coughing seawater into his sleeve. "I've always prayed to him. Every day. Maybe I did something in a past life to please him... My brother... please, my brother is back there."

I met his eyes, even though the pain in them made me want to drop my gaze to the ice. "Your brother will be gone by now. I'm sorry."

"There are a lot of men there," he protested. "You don't know... please. He has ginger hair and a scarf—"

I held up my hand to stop him. My soul ached for him. I knew what it was like to lose family. But I had to be firm. "Even if the whales haven't gotten him, the water is freezing. By the time I get to him and bring him here, he'll be too frozen to recover."

"But—"

"I'm not from Aegir," I said, cutting him off. "I made a deal with Loki. I want to make one with you, too."

The sailor bit his lip. "You made a deal with the trickster? But everyone knows... everyone knows how dangerous that is."

"I know that now." My voice was flat. I didn't want to elaborate. I didn't want to tell this man just how deeply I regretted dealing with Loki, because just saying the words might rip me in half.

He closed his eyes and took a deep, ragged breath. Pain frosted his voice when he spoke, "And now, I suppose, in order to live, I have to make a deal with Loki as well."

I tried to sound nonchalant and keep the desperation in my voice at bay. I hoped he would ask for something straightforward, something easy that Loki couldn't manipulate. "I already saved you. I'm hardly going to push you back in the water."

He shrugged. "I'll freeze to death here unless another ship comes by. I want to live to see my family again."

"Others have survived," I snapped.

The sailor turned his head from side to side, studying the barren landscape. He rubbed the back of his head and gave a hollow laugh. "They either had help or fins."

I pursed my lips. I couldn't sit here and talk about Ragna and life on the ice with him. The longer we spoke, the harder my task would get. Even if I saved him from the ocean and the whales, I still needed to use him. I pulled one of the enchanted vials from the string around my neck. My hand rested on the cork as I pondered how Loki might distort this man's request.

The sailor looked at me in hopeful terror. He knew the legends. I imagined Loki transforming him into a seagull or a pelican, able to soar above the waves and fly back to his homeland, but cursed to look at his family from above. He'd be able to watch them from afar, to nest in their roof, but never interact with them.

"I need your voice." My own voice almost died as I fought to get the words out. Somehow, I would find a way to get this man home in his human form. He would see his family. He would hold them again.

His trembling hand went to his throat. "You'll send me home a mute?"

"In exchange, I promise I will keep you safe and fed until the next ship comes. Your deal will be with me. Loki will not have to grant you anything. I will keep you alive."

"My daughter is blind."

Suddenly I couldn't speak. Grief and guilt threatened to swallow me. How could I do that to him? To his little girl? But if I didn't, I could be trapped like this forever.

"She won't know me," the man continued, shattering me again and again with every word. "She won't even know that I came back."

"She'll know you by other things, by the feel of your face, your smell," I said, even as guilt threatened to strangle me. I hoped that was true. I needed to believe it was true. Human senses were different from ours; perhaps they relied on vision where we did not.

His eyes scanned the length of my body, from my hair to the tips of my tentacles. "You need this, don't you?"

I nodded.

"What were you, before?"

I sighed, bracing myself for disbelief. "A mermaid."

He smiled although sadness lingered in his dark eyes. "Well, your top still looks the same, and I bet you were beautiful. How many favors did you bestow? Break many sailors' hearts?"

I tossed my hair over my shoulder and tried to keep my voice light. "All the time."

We sat in silence. His teeth chattered, and he rubbed his hands together and blew into his palms. I wrapped two of my tentacles around his back and forced more heat to the surface of my scales. He sighed as the heat penetrated his wet furs.

Brushing a lock of wet hair from his face, he closed his eyes and pried the vial from my locked fingers. "You saved me. I repay my debts. Somehow, I will find a way to convince my girl I'm still there for her. Without you, that's a promise I couldn't keep."

He pulled out the vial's cork with his teeth. Fingers shaking, he raised the little bottle in a mocking toast as liquid silver frothed from his lips.

When it was over, his great shoulders shook, and tears fell in rivers down his cheeks, but not a sound passed his lips.

*   *   *

I watched the sailor, guarded him and fed him for eight days, until the next ship cruised through. I had no way of knowing whether the men who took him aboard were his countrymen or not, but they wrapped a blanket around his shoulders and forced a bowl of something that steamed into his fingers the moment he climbed aboard. Then a man decorated with gray and blue feathers herded him below deck. I watched the ship until it sailed out of sight. Then I crept back to my den and waited for the trickster to seek me out.

I didn't have to wait long. I had no sooner laid back on my spongy pallet, when Loki slipped under the cabin door. They flattened their body like a sandfish and oozed through the tiny crevice. Silver oil rose in the water as they materialized into a solid form.

Tonight, they chose the body of a human woman, a woman dressed for an occasion. They wore their long hair in curled rivulets that remained dry and springy, though we were more than sixty arm-lengths under the sea. A shimmering green dress clung to their silhouette almost like scales. The dress fanned out delicately at the ankles to reveal shoes made entirely from mother-of-pearl. If they weren't such a monster, I would have said they were beautiful.

Loki stumbled to my table and lifted the vial filled with the sailor's voice. They opened it, and then drank the voice like thick milk. When Loki spoke, the sailor's voice spilled out, but it was tainted by what was inside them and the low gravel came out like a hiss. "You made your own deal with the human. That wasn't what we agreed."

"We never agreed anything about that," I said, returning their glare. "The deal we struck was simple. I bring you three voices: one creature, one human, one merperson. In exchange, you give me what I ask before I give you the third voice. We didn't negotiate any more specifics than that."

Loki cursed, slamming their delicate-looking fist on the table. The old, sodden wood caved under the impact, and splinters floated into the space around us. I cringed. "Be careful, little mermaid. Remember that you are dealing with a god, and I could crush the life from your body with a snap of my fingers."

"I don't forget what I am dealing with," I said quietly.

"You'll never finish this bargain anyway," they sneered. "This summer looks like it will be a long one. A few years at the least. The merfolk are looking for a new ice mountain, farther to the north. You'll be all alone here. Who knows if you'll live to see them return."

A dull ache pulsed in my chest. I wanted to taunt them, and remind them that I'd bested them twice now. But if the merfolk had started migrating, then my chances of success were dwindling. I had to risk sneaking into the glacier again. "You're not the god of fate. You can't predict the future."

Loki's nostrils flared. They jabbed an elegant finger at me. "I'll see you rot here. Wouldn't that be something? A monster's corpse, buried here amongst the bones of the humans she loved so much?"

Three

Loki left me with that final taunt. The hollow ache spread through my whole body. Even my rogue tentacles lay limp by my sides. I had little time to find a merperson to help me. The idea of waiting years, trapped inside this hulk with no one… it made me want to impale myself on the human sword in the corner. I was willing to spend my dying breaths wriggling like a worm on a human fishing hook until the blade pierced my heart.

I slept fitfully, dozing in and out of consciousness until the water lightened with the morning sun. Even then, I couldn't motivate myself to leave my bed. So I counted cracks in the weathered wooden ceiling and tried to find some meaning in my situation.

In many of our legends, Loki was depicted with a sense of humor. When I was young, all the storytellers talked about them as if they were a jovial prankster—not to be trusted, of course—but not exactly evil either, just a being that lived for their own entertainment and didn't care who got hurt in the process. When I turned thirteen and Mama had allowed me to stay to hear the stories the bards only told the adults, I'd learned about Loki in a different light. The god of lies enjoyed pain and didn't care if their bargains ruined lives or caused deaths.

My own experience told me that the misery of lost hope pleased the god above all else. Loki promised the world and delivered hell, but here I was, still striving to meet their conditions.

I rolled over and buried my face in the seaweed cushion that grew from the decaying pallet. The seaweed smelled sweet and grew thicker by the day. Algae covered the walls, and a family of sand crabs had made their home in the drawers next to the bed. It seemed that the heat emanating from my scales had brought life to the ship, reviving the titan from its deathly slumber in a kind of reincarnation.

Someone tapped on the door. I thought I must have imagined it, but the sound came again, louder and more insistent. It had to be Loki, probably ready to forge a new deal and try to bind me closer to him. He knew that despite my small successes, I still had the hardest challenge left, and my hope was fading. If I didn't try to complete Loki's tasks, what would be the fun for the god? Maybe they would let me die in peace if I became too boring. I turned over on my stomach and blocked my ears with my hands. They would come in anyway, no matter what I said.

"Ersel?"

Tears sprang to my eyes. The trick was too cruel. Even for Loki.

"Ersel?" The voice repeated. "Please. Please just let me in. This is the first chance I've had to sneak away. King Calder has had me under guard. I only managed to come because they assigned Havamal to me... and he turned a blind eye."

Against all my judgment, I swam to the door. A storm of emotions flowed through my body, and when I reached for the knob my hand buzzed as if with lightning. I sucked down a deep gulp of water and slowly turned the handle.

And flung myself into the arms of my mother.

She felt smaller. Her arms were strong, but shaking, around my back. She'd always struggled to wrap her arms all the way around my back, but now her elbows sagged behind me with inches to spare. She pushed me back and looked into my face. I studied her. Her cheeks looked hollow, and her eyes were set deep in their sockets. I wondered what I must look like.

"Thank the gods," she whispered. "I thought I might be too late."

I didn't dare to ask her what she had imagined I would do. The relief at seeing her was so great that all I could do was stare.

She picked up a heavy basket and held it out to me. "Havamal helped me get this. It's not much, but there are some of your favorites. I know I shouldn't defend him. I don't think he would want me to defend him either, but he's been helpful to me. He's looked after me when he could."

I pushed the lid back, and my mouth watered. The basket overflowed with seahorse jerky, sweetened kelp, and shark fin. I lifted one of the seahorses to my lips and tore off its succulent head with my teeth. Havamal remembered. The thought both pleased and hurt me. I might never forgive him, but it was nice to know our friendship had had once been real.

Mama took a seat on the edge of the table and watched me with a half-smile as I devoured the food.

"I'm here to make a deal."

My eyes widened and the food dropped from my hands as I processed what she was saying. "No. No you can't. You can't be serious."

"Are you telling your mother what to do now, Ersel?" She tried to smile, tried to wink, but all I could see in her eyes was exhaustion.

"Loki is a monster."

She nodded. "I know that. I can see what they've done to you, and I was there at Vigdis's delivery…"

I held my breath waiting for her to continue, but she didn't. My imagination began to conjure the baby's appearance: a monstrosity, with Vigdis's coral fins, tusks protruding from its mouth, and hundreds of unblinking eyes covering its torso—sad, haunted eyes, all of them like Vigdis's own eyes had looked during my trial.

"It died," Mama said at last. I breathed a sigh of relief, and Mama pressed her lips together before saying, "So did she. It really scared a lot of merfolk… and they're scared not just of Loki, but of King Calder as well. Of his plans for our girls. Havamal's been speaking with some… it's amazing how many girls feel trapped, but would never admit it."

Self-disgust welled in me. I'd done all this for a chance at my freedom; I'd thought myself alone in my hatred for our system. My selfishness, my belief that I was somehow different and all alone, had gotten Vigdis killed. It may have been Loki who had sent the beast that killed her, but her blood was on my hands, too. How many other mermaids were like me, silently going through the motions, cursing their fate and limited options, before finally succumbing to something they believed was inevitable? Maybe if I survived this deal with Loki, I could do something to help them. I squashed the thought almost as quickly as it arose. There was nothing I could possibly do against the king.

Mama's sharp eyes scanned the room until they fell on the last remaining vial. One of my tentacles darted out to stop her, but she slapped the end of it and picked the little bottle up, rotating it in her hand. "How many do you have left to collect?"

"Just one more," I whispered.

"One more and you're free?"

"I hope to be."

Mama looked up to the ceiling. "I pray to Loki. I want to make a deal."

Tears fell down my cheeks as fast as rain in a storm. The water around us warmed with my emotions. "Stop, Mama. Stop! You can't; they'll destroy you."

Mama set her mouth in a firm line. "I've had two months to think about this."

"Whatever you want, they'll distort it. They'll make it ugly and nothing like you expect. They just want to cause misery." I begged her.

When at first no one came, I dared to hope that her invocation wouldn't work. Maybe Loki simply wasn't interested in my mother; maybe they sensed in her a moral fiber they couldn't corrupt. Mama was the child of the Spring Rains, after all, the daughter of Ran and Frigga. Maybe they simply didn't want to tangle with the other gods.

But then electric green sludge began seeping from the ceiling, moving against the water as if it were simply air. It poured into the room and filled it with bright green light.

Loki materialized; a frozen grin stretched across their face. They appeared as such a perfect replica of the king that I had to resist the urge to fall to the floor. The shift was perfect, down to every wrinkle around King Calder's eyes and the exact glint of his scales, though a pale green haze lingered in the water around his outline.

Cloud-gray eyes flashing with mischief, Loki clutched a bone trident and brandished it with glee. "What a sentimental addition to my collection of curiosities. A mother-daughter pair! I should have expected something like this. Some sort of silly sacrifice. What's it to be? I let her go? I keep you instead? That kind of usual parental nonsense?"

Before Mama could speak, I cut in desperately. I couldn't let them twist her words. I couldn't. "She is my last voice. Her deal is with me."

"You can't lie to me. I invented it." Loki's hands balled into fists. "She invoked me. She'll make her bargain with me, and then you and I can see about settling our last voice."

"To bear witness." I crossed my arms over my chest. "Our deal comes first. And if you go back on it, the other gods will put things to rights. I know the legends."

They snickered. The green haze swirled around the god, and in a blink their form shifted into the lithe warrior I had seen at our first meeting. "Am I like the legends you know? Haven't I surprised you enough yet? What makes you think your precious legends know anything about the way the gods work?"

Their question made me hesitate. I wanted to snatch the vial from Mama's hands. I wanted her to swim away as fast as she could to a place where I might never see her again, a place where even Loki could never find her.

But a small, selfish part of me, at war with everything else, wanted her to save me.

Mama uncorked the bottle. Our eyes met, and I saw the trust in her gaze as well as the plea for me to trust her. She was putting her fate in my hands, trusting that we could save each other.

Loki smiled. "And what do you want in return?"

Mama's fingers hesitated; the vial was just inches from her lips. "You can grant anything?"

The god chuckled. "I've changed the outcomes of battles, brought lovers back from the dead. I'm a god. So yes, mortal, anything your mind can conceive."

"I want my child to be happy," she said. "Truly happy, not in a forced state or something mind-controlled. I want you to give her the things that will make her happiest in the world."

My hand went to my mouth.

"That's too abstract," Loki said, shaking their horned head. "You have to ask for something real. Something I can understand. Happiness isn't a thing I can just give. It's not an outcome. It's a condition of every moment."

"Then you'll have to grant her something in every one of them." Mama braced her hands on her wide hips. "Perhaps it will do you good to think of another's happiness in every second of your life."

Loki and I stared. I'd never had so much admiration for her.

"You're a god. You've been alive for millennia. I'm sure 'abstract' is something you can overcome. If you cannot fulfill our deal..." Mama trailed off.

Loki snarled. Moving so fast their body blurred, their hands were on my throat. I gasped and spluttered as strong fingers crushed my windpipe. "How did you get her to come here? How did you do it? You cheated somehow, I know it." Dropping me, they rounded on my mother. "Maybe your daughter will find happiness, but you will be an outcast. You're here against your king's wishes, against your all your laws."

"I know the repercussions of the choice I'm making." Mama's jaw stiffened. "And my voice is not the part of me I value the most. That part grew up a long time ago. She's standing right in front of me."

Loki glared at her before smoothing their hair back. "I won't give you that deal."

Above us, I heard hail fall on the surface, followed by the clap of thunder.

"You said, 'anything,'" my mother reminded him. "You already gave your conditions."

Loki paled, and something like confidence grew inside me. The legends were true. The fear in their face told me as much. They would have to keep their promise. Thunder struck. I imagined Thor surfing on the waves and holding his hammer outstretched as he descended to bring justice. Loki and I looked up.

When I turned back to my mother, she held the bottle out to me, filled with the pearl white liquid. Her hand pressed against her throat, and when she mouthed, 'I love you,' I heard nothing and everything. In my hands, I clutched the third and final voice.

Loki held out their hand.

Trembling, I took the bottle from Mama. My whole body crawled with fear. I had the thing he wanted. I could ask for whatever I wanted and I had learned to be specific.

I cradled the vial against my chest. Mama had given up her voice, but I was the one who didn't know what to say.

Thunder cracked overhead. The gods were impatient. They wanted to see the deal fulfilled so they could turn their attention elsewhere. The vial felt warm against my scales; it was comforting in a way none of the others had been. I could almost hear Mama hum a soothing lullaby within the milky liquid.

With the attention of all of Asgard on me, I took a chance. The god of lies might kill me where I stood, but I had to take the chance. "Our deal is complete."

"Yes, yes. Nearly. Give me the bottle."

I hugged Mama's voice closer to my chest; my heart beat so hard it threatened to escape up my throat. "Our deal is complete. I brought you three voices. It was never stated that I had to actually give them to you."

I wouldn't have dared to try something so brazen before; I feared Loki's wrath. If it had been anyone else's voice in my hands, I still might never have dared. But Mama had stood up to them and her stubbornness gave me the courage I needed.

Loki lunged for me. The bottle slipped from my fingers, but they focused entirely on me. Their eyes glowed red, and heat emanated from them. I shut my eyes, knowing this was the end. I waited for them to kill me.

The water in the room flashed as lightning struck the surface of the water.

"Our deal is complete," I whispered a final time.

They glanced up to the ceiling, then jabbed a thick finger at me. "This isn't over. You've made an enemy of a god."

"You're right, it's not over," Mama said, and I almost cried at the sweet sound of her voice. "Ersel is owed something in return. Her choice."

I could ask Loki for the legs I'd wanted all along, so that I could search the lands for Ragna and a new fortune. I spoke the *godstongue*, and perhaps someone would have heard of her. We could find our freedom together. I would learn to build, to construct things the way humans did, and engineer a new a life for myself away from the archaic rituals of the glacier.

I had always wanted something more. With her willingness to sacrifice herself, Mama presented me with a second chance.

But as the wish tickled my tongue, I bit down on it. Loki crossed their arms over their chest. A fresh smirk twitched at the corners of their lips as if they were daring me.

But my home... Vigdis was dead, and in the wake of my departure others like me had come forward to tell Havamal their stories. Vigdis and I had never been friends, but if I took this chance and left the other mermaids to the fate I feared more than anything, my guilt might destroy me. My tentacles were strangely still; the gaping mouths were at rest.

All I had to do was ask Loki to change me back, to give me the fins I'd hated and now longed for. The words stuck in my throat. I couldn't be selfish, not after what Mama had been willing to do.

"Tell me how to change it," I said, meeting the god's green-rimmed stare. "Tell me how to get rid of these laws, the king... tell me how to change things so that no one else has to feel like I did. Tell me how to stop all this suffering."

Loki's turquoise eyebrows shot up. "What?" they asked, shock evident in their tone. "After all of this, you're telling me you don't want legs? You don't want me to do anything? You just want answers?"

I raised my chin. "If I ask for answers, then I'm the one who decides what to do with them. The outcome is outside your control."

"What of your human love?" The god's eyes laughed at me. "All this to reunite with her, to be on land and be together, and what, you're just going to forget about her?"

They were right. I would never forget Ragna, and I would cling to the fruitless hope that one day she might come back. But I set my jaw and crossed my arms over my chest. Although every part of me itched to slap them, I knew it would make Loki angrier if I refused to rise to their baiting.

"You're just like the king. You don't understand me at all," I said, shrugging and taking the tiniest step toward them. "If you think I did all this for her."

For a moment, I felt the ghost of Ragna's kiss heating my lips, but when I blinked I felt only scalding tears sliding under my lashes and making their way to my chin. Then I whispered, "It was about something more than that."

Loki's gaze bore into mine; the color of their irises shifted from kelp green to storm-cloud gray. Deep in their soulless depths, I saw a flicker of respect. "King Calder's sister, the princess Inkeri… she lives."

Behind me, Mama gasped.

I stared at him. The information was at once so simple, unexpected, and powerful. The king's sister, our rightful queen, whom everyone thought had died, was alive? Where had she been for the last ten years? I tried to picture the princess of my childhood. Inkeri had been fragile, sickly, and always in her brother's shadow. But she'd had gentle eyes, fins the color of brilliant sunshine, and a quick smile for anyone who spoke to her. Although the fortress had mourned, no one had trouble believing it when she perished.

"Where?" I demanded. I had too many questions, but with Loki I wanted to keep them as simple as I could so they couldn't twist things. How had the king hidden her all these years? And why had he done it? Inkeri had been his puppet, doing whatever her brother asked without the smallest hint of a rebellious nature. "Is she in the fortress?"

"Oh, no," Loki said, grinning as if they took pleasure in whatever hellish predicament King Calder had devised for his sister. "He made her a special pit. He goes there to feed her himself, through a window just large enough to slip a wee basket in. He's been building the walls thicker by the year. By now, you'd probably need fire to blast through them."

"Why not just kill her?" Mama asked, as she rose from my bed and swam over to us. "I know the king is a sadist, but it seems an unnecessary risk to keep her alive."

Loki laughed, and their eyes lit with something like joy. "However distantly, the royal lines of the merfolk are linked to Aegir; they descend from the product of an indiscretion in his wilder youth. The sea god is a lazy hedonist who takes little interest in the power of his second sight. Most of the time Aegir does not concern himself with what you merfolk do to each other. He's much more invested in the orcas and the sharks.

However, when one of his own line dies, he feels the soul's departure."

Our legends said that the gods cursed fratricide above all else. While I doubted Loki condemned any crime, the sea god was rumored to enforce the sacred laws with severity when he bothered to take an interest. I tried to imagine what life had been like for Inkeri, alone and sealed in the deep, probably knowing that everyone believed her dead. It was a fate worse than anything I had imagined for myself. Now that I knew the truth, I had to help her. It was the only way to begin to atone for what had happened to Vigdis.

"Where is the pit?"

"Near the shark bay, in the iceberg just off the north point of the ice shelf." Seeming to assess my reactions, Loki watched me while I thought. "You won't be able to free her. The ice around her is much too thick."

"I didn't ask for your opinion," I snapped. The fact that the god hadn't yet dissolved me into a splash of green oil loosened my tongue. "Just for information."

Their eyes twinkled, and a grin tugged at the corners of their lips. "I want to give you a gift."

I backed away from them, taking Mama's hand. "I don't want your gifts."

The god pressed a hand to their left breast and wobbled on their feet; the mocking smile was in place once more. "You wound me. No, this isn't a bargain. If you do not like the gift I give you, then you may return it at any time. But you have passed my test. I consider you worthy of my rare blessing."

Test? I nearly lunged for them, wanting to gouge Loki's eyes out and rip the teeth from their smug mouth. In these months of torture, they'd been testing me?

"A test? A test for what? What is wrong with you?"

Loki shrugged. "Many pray to me but few are worthy of my interest or my true assistance. You mortals think very highly of your value to us. I choose my followers carefully, but when I have chosen, I can be a valuable ally. Once you've had time to think and adjust, I will return."

"You killed Vigdis as part of a test?" I seethed.

The god shrugged. "She was a useless girl."

"She was a child!" Mama interrupted. "She didn't even have time to know herself, much less see what she could become."

Loki shrugged. "Ersel did not have to choose her. She did not have to accept my deal at all."

With those words, they pushed a blade straight into my heart. The trickster rubbed their hands together and green sludge erupted from the tips of their fingers, spraying me like ink from a spooked squid. The liquid stank of dead flesh and decay. I screamed, waiting for the pain I was sure would follow and trying to scrub the slime from my skin. It began to seep in through my pores.

"I don't agree to this!" I screamed, clawing at my flesh. "This is not a bargain. Odin, Freya—"

Loki inspected their long nails, as if judging their sharpness. "Oh, stop it. Odin won't intervene. He knows you'll like this. And as you said, it's not a deal. It's my gift to you."

When all of the green slime had oozed in through my skin, I looked at myself, assessing the change. I didn't look or feel any different. The eight monstrous legs still lurked beneath my torso, each casually exploring the room by touch, each compelled by a will all its own.

Loki crossed their arms and leaned against the fragile wood of the human closet. "I have given you three forms. When you learn to show me a little gratitude, I'll give you more."

"Gratitude?" I spat out. "You honestly expect me to thank you after everything you've put me through?"

"Forms?" Mama asked, looking at Loki as if she wanted to dismember them. Her fingers grasped one of the rust-dulled blades from the tabletop. After what I'd seen her do, it wouldn't surprise me to see her embed it in Loki's back. "What forms? What are you talking about?"

Loki held up three slender fingers and counted them off. "This beast, which you may inhabit to remind you of your folly. Merperson. Human. You will now be able to shift between them. They all belong to you, and I am sure you will find uses for all of them."

My breath stopped. After all my months of struggle, they'd just given me the human form I had desired when I made that first, horrible deal that had sealed Vigdis's fate and led to all of this. Rage burst from me in an explosion of flying tentacles. I hit the god again and again, focusing pure anger on them as my legs bombarded their head, back, and sides.

When they recovered from the shock, Loki straightened and made a fist in the air. Immediately, my tentacles stilled as if bound to my body by an invisible chord. They pulled an empty vial from their sleeve and pressed it into my shaking hand. "Use this to shift. It is an object forged by me and will help you activate what is inside you."

I turned the bottle over in my hand. A small chain was attached to each of its sides, just long enough for me to wear around my arm like a bracelet... or a fetter. I had to resist the urge to bash it against the door and crush the vial to pieces.

The trickster cleared their throat, then said, "As I said, I will allow you time to settle, but I will be back. If you'd been a good girl and accepted your gift nicely, I might not have made you use a talisman." They grinned and I struggled against the binding force. "But... I see you still have some learning to do. I've made an investment in you, in your training, and I don't like to waste my time."

Striding toward the door, Loki pulled it open and vanished in a flood of emerald light.

When the rusted door closed, Mama and I exchanged looks.

Wincing as if the metal burned my skin, I wrapped the chain of Loki's gift around my wrist. I would think before I decided to destroy it. Whatever the vial contained was just as likely to curse me as bless me, but I was afraid of what Loki might do if they learned I had destroyed something so valuable.

"I'll be back," I said. "I want to check outside. I want to see..."

I didn't finish my sentence, but Mama nodded, understanding my need to be alone and free after so much time bound to Loki's whim. I'd find her later, and we would have all the time in the world to catch up and then plan what to do, now that we knew the rightful heir to our glacier's throne was still alive.

I look around outside to make sure the god had truly vanished before pushing off the ship's deck into the ocean. I didn't want Mama to watch me try my two other "forms" in case this was another of Loki's elaborate jokes—something they'd devised to give me temporary hope, just to see any shard of optimism in me dashed.

Once I was sure I'd gone far enough, I looked at the tentacles, bidding them goodbye. I shut my eyes and willed them to transform, but nothing happened. I expected a puff of green ink, or for something to swallow me up and spit me out in a new body. Even though the vial had been a gift and not something I'd earned, disappointment curled around my abdomen, squeezing as tightly as Loki's sea serpent had done during our first meeting.

I still held the tiny vial. I looked at it and then turned it over with distaste. Loki had said it would tie me to them and activate my powers. I didn't want any lingering bond with the sadistic god. Of course, Loki had known that when they gave me the new power. I clenched my fingers so tightly that I nearly shattered the little vial.

How would I activate it? Knowing the god's ego, it probably involved a prayer or request to them. Loki would want to listen to me plead.

"I am not making a bargain with you." I hissed into the open water. "With Odin as my witness, you gave this to me of your own volition."

I sighed, hating myself as I whispered a soft invocation with my lips against the bottle. Even if I never used it again, I wanted my speed, my agility, and, if I was honest with myself, my beauty, to return.

Turquoise oil formed a perfumed cloud around me. It smelled sweet as baby kelp and sounded like the whisper of a summer ocean I could barely remember. When it diffused, I looked down and my heart leapt into my throat. My fins and tail were back, but they were different, enhanced. Before, my scales had been shades of royal blue, but now beautiful white and lilac scales were mixed among the palest shade of sky blue. My tail gleamed and shimmered like a pearl held to the light. Each fin was tapered and translucent and looked as delicate as the softest sea-silk. But I could feel the strength in them.

This tail would forever mark me as different, special. No one else under the ocean had such scales. Would that make me something to treasure or something to hunt?

Loki was bribing me, trying their hardest to make me feel gratitude, as if I could forget the horrors of the past months. I wouldn't let myself be drawn into their snare again. I would take this gift and use it, but I would never agree to do anything for the trickster.

Wearing a smile that stretched my jaw, I flipped, pivoted, and spun, relishing the feeling of my nimble tail and streamlined fins. The storm above had cleared, and sunlight filtered through the water, making creatures from dancing light. The ocean stretched out around me, blue and endless.

Four

I SWAM FOR THE SURFACE, making my body streamlined as an elegant harpoon. My new fins burned as I pushed them to the limit of their speed. I knew I couldn't go back to the glacier, and I hated the idea of going back to my lonely sea cabin. Leaping into the air, I let the sunlight kiss my scales. I landed backward in the water, whooping with delight at the way the light made the pearl white sections of my new tail gleam brighter than fresh snow.

"Wow," said a soft voice from someone swimming up behind me. I whirled, faster than I'd ever been able to spin before. "Your Mama told me about Loki's gift, but..."

Havamal offered me a shy half-smile that didn't quite reach his tired eyes. Though his muscular chest was as broad as it had ever been, he looked smaller somehow, hunched. Deep exhaustion seemed to cling to his graying skin. My jubilant best friend was truly gone.

Whatever he had done to me, I wasn't shielded from his misery. The pit of my stomach dropped. I had to find some way to move forward. Holding on to grudges would only bring both of us pain. I threw my arms around him. His body went rigid at the unexpected embrace; his arms hung limp against his sides. Then, he patted my back and lowered his head to rest atop mine.

"I'm sorry," he whispered into my hair. "Erie, you have to understand. I am so sorry."

"I know. I'm not sure I will ever truly forgive you," I said, squeezing him a little tighter. I looked up into his face and took his chin between my fingers. He looked away, averting his hurt eyes from mine. "But I'm willing to try to forget it. I can't be your lover. Never. Not after what happened. But I can try to be your friend again."

His muscles tensed, and he hugged me to his chest so tightly that he drove the air from my lungs. I sagged against him, letting him do the work of keeping us level in the water. "I'll spend the rest of my life trying to make it up to you."

I smiled at him. "From what Mama tells me, you've already started."

Havamal released me and nodded gravely. "I've started talking to some of the others. You're not alone in how you felt. I guess I never realized how afraid The Grading made all of you. We were always told the birthing area was peaceful, natural." He shook his head and snorted with disgust. "I can't believe I bought all of that. I should have known better than to believe the king."

I looked around us, surveying the open ocean for any other listening ears. Sound could travel a long way beneath the sea, and kelp grew everywhere, providing natural places to hide. It was a risk to share secrets when it was hard to tell whether you were truly alone. In Havamal's ear, I whispered, "Did my Mama tell you the rest of it? What I asked Loki?"

"No. She told me there was more, but she didn't dare tell me inside the glacier," he said quietly against my cheek. "And I have a secret for you as well."

"The king's sister is alive."

Havamal let me go. We drifted apart minutely while he gaped at me. "Inkeri? The princess?"

I nodded. "He's been keeping her in an iceberg off the north point all this time."

He sucked in a breath. "What? How? How did he get away with it?"

"He feeds her himself. Goes there alone."

Havamal swore. He swam back and forth, nearly growling. "That's where he goes… every afternoon the king 'retreats'… he won't let any of us accompany him. He says he needs to clear his head. When I first started, I used to argue, because we're kept to guard him. What is the point if he just wanders away? He had me whipped the second time I asked about it."

"And no one has ever followed him?" I demanded. "He's been doing this for ten years. Not one of you has ever—"

"Once," Havamal interrupted. His eyes hardened as he recollected. "One of the guards did. Rala."

"The super quiet one with the black scales?" I remembered Rala. He usually stood by the door during the midday meals. He always stood with his arms crossed and remained silent while his sharp eyes took in everything.

"He has no tongue," Havamal said, swallowing hard. "He's so quiet because he has no tongue. The king cut it out. I don't even think he saw anything. There never was a trial."

"That's vile." I wrapped my arms around myself, shivering. Going up against King Calder would have to be planned carefully. Given what he had done to his own sister, I knew he wouldn't hesitate to destroy us if we ever gave him the upper hand. "Loki said that the king has been building the ice wall thicker by the year. I'm not sure how we can break it. We'd need more heat than any of us could possibly generate with our scales. They said we'd need human fire."

A crooked grin appeared on Havamal's face. This time his eyes sparkled too. "My surprise might be able to help with that."

*   *   *

DESPITE MY PROTESTS, HAVAMAL REFUSED to give me any details as he led me to his waiting surprise. He ripped a long, flexible strip of kelp from one of the stalks as we swam over it. When he started to tie it around my eyes, I crossed my arms over my chest but didn't make a move to stop him. After the blindfold was secured, calm settled over me. Havamal couldn't see my eyes now, couldn't read all the conflicting thoughts and feelings behind them.

The idea of a gift or a surprise scratched my already raw emotions, which were barely kept in check. It reminded me of things he'd done a hundred times when we were children, and the nostalgia hurt when it should have brought me joy. Through the kelp blindfold, I could see only the barest hint of shadows. Havamal took my hand to guide me.

When we stopped swimming, Havamal lifted my hand above my head. With my heart racing, I felt around until my fingers rested on something solid. I touched wood that had been blasted smooth by waves and salt. A film of algae covered a hull, which felt thin and grainy, suggesting the ship had sailed in colder waters for quite some time.

I sighed and reached behind my head to undo the blindfold. "Did you bring me back to a wreck? I told you, I want to move forward, but I'm going to need some time... dredging up old memories isn't going to work."

Grunting, Havamal snatched the blindfold. I blinked and looked up. A great ship floated above us, swaying gently on the waves. An iron anchor attached by a long, rusting chain kept the giant in place. Havamal surfaced, and I followed, wide-eyed. Why had the ship dropped its anchor? I couldn't see any holes in the bottom, and, with the drifting icebergs all around, it didn't seem like a good idea for the humans to linger.

I kept my head low in the water, surveying the vessel. I could tell that it was a different type of ship than the titans the humans used to hunt whales. It had a shallower hold and a narrower frame. The side rails and interior rested just five or six feet above the surface of the ocean, and dozens of oars extended from the deck. Brightly colored sigils depicting beasts I'd never seen or imagined were painted atop the rails.

Havamal knocked on the side of the hull; he drummed a distinct rhythm that no one would ever mistake for a shark or whale. Feet, slow to move, shuffled on the deck, and a groggy female voice commanded, "Check what's over the starboard."

A ginger head peered over the edge of the ship. The man scowled; a broken tooth jutted between his lips. Then he turned and shouted over his shoulder. "It's that merman again. The one with the silver tail."

Heavy footfalls clattered across the deck. Elegantly, the female swung her leg over the side of the ship and sat on the rail. Blonde hair whipped in the gusting wind and wild eyes bore into Havamal, as if the girl were getting ready to thrust a spear into his side.

For a moment, my heart stopped. Suddenly I didn't know whether to burst into tears or laughter.

Ragna's skeletal frame had filled out, her cheeks were flushed, and her body had grown solid with muscle. Metal weapons were strapped to every inch of her: a pair of crossed swords over her chest, blades peeking from her boots, a quiver of arrows slung over her shoulder. But it was the gleaming silver hook extending from her stump of an arm that drew my attention. One of her delicate, long-fingered hands was gone, and jagged scars ran up her slender arm, overlaying her moving tattoos.

She brandished the hook at Havamal. "I told you that if you came back here, I'd put this through your cheek and drag you behind the boat like a tuna fish."

Havamal folded his arms over his broad chest and gestured to me. I was still barely peeking out of the water, hardly daring to look up. I knew my lapis hair made me difficult to spot against the sunlit waves. Ragna squinted, then stiffened, her intact hand gripping the edge of the ship so hard her knuckles went white.

I kicked my tail harder, raising myself from the water a bit more. Ragna's eyes softened. Her lips curved into a smile. I felt light enough to fly. She came back. She actually came back. The ice grip on my heart started to thaw.

Gripping the little vial, I said the invocation to the trickster and shifted back into my monstrous form. As I formed the words, a little punch went through my gut; I hated what I had to say in order to use this beautiful and terrible power. But all I wanted was to get to Ragna in the ship. I didn't care what she saw as long as I could reach her. The mouths on my tentacles gripped the ship's sturdy side, and I climbed aboard with ease.

As I scuttled onto the deck, men jumped from their benches. Fear was evident on their faces, though they looked like seasoned warriors and all carried an assortment of lethal weapons. Most of them had visible scars covering bodies lean with hard muscle. Each of them looked as war-ready as the ship. I wondered where Ragna had found this crew and what had happened to her while we'd been apart, what had left her both maimed and in power.

Tightly gripping the vial as the warriors lifted their weapons, I shifted into my human form for the first time. The nearest human, a boy who could not have been older than his teens judging by his lanky frame and acne-scarred cheeks, flushed red. A few others let out loud exclamations. Some turned away and muttered.

"Shit, lass," said a grizzled bear of a man to my left. "These boys don't need to be thinking about that in their bunks. None of us will get any sleep."

Ragna let out a shriek of pure delight that silenced the rest of the crew. Freezing air kissed my scale-less body and I nearly cried out from its intensity. I lifted a slender leg and marveled at its elegant line, at the markless perfection of my new skin, not boring at all despite the lack of ink and scales. Ragna removed her heavy fur cloak and wrapped it around me. It was impossibly soft against my newborn skin and stopped the cold from blistering me.

In the water, Havamal laughed. It was a genuine laugh, deep and full. Then I heard a splash, and his head disappeared under the waves. I didn't notice I was smiling until a gust of wind stung my exposed teeth. Dizzy giddiness made my knees weak and my head light.

"Witchery," murmured one of the crew's older men. "Damn witchery. I knew this placed was cursed."

"Is she the sea goddess?" The teenager demanded.

"No thousand-year-old sea goddess looks like that, dunderwit."

"We should push her overboard."

"I want to push her into my bunk."

"Can all krakens do that?"

All the men around us began speculating at once. I shrank closer to Ragna, not yet sure what to make of all these humans.

Ignoring her crew, Ragna pulled me into a small shelter that was enclosed on three sides. The wooden shack blocked some of the wind, but I couldn't stop shivering. Even with Ragna's fur shielding my nakedness, I felt a deeper cold than I had ever known, a chill that radiated right down to my bones. The men turned on their benches, straining to catch our words.

Her silver hook glinted in the sun. I lifted her maimed arm. She flinched and her nose curled in distaste as she tried to pull it away from me.

"What happened?" I asked, feeling both the heaviness of what she had lost and relief that I was not the only one who had changed, whose body betrayed the truth of past horrors. She had a ship now, and men who answered to her. I couldn't help the pang of longing that ran through me. While I'd been trapped in Loki's game, she'd forged a new future for herself.

She shrugged, raising her dark brown eyes to mine. "I got my revenge, but this was the price. I found the man who wanted to take me and I killed him." Gesturing at my legs with a sly half-smile, she asked, "What happened? And what was with the kraken moves earlier?"

I bit my lip, wondering how much to tell her now. Eventually, I would tell her all about Loki, about what I'd done and the months I'd spent trying to fix it. Her eyes were bright, and I didn't want sadness to dim them, not yet, so I whispered, "I got my freedom. That was the price."

We just stared at each other, trying to imagine and understand. Then Ragna crouched and flipped open a hatch beneath our feet. "Let's get out of the wind," she said. Gesturing at the crew, she rolled her eyes. "And somewhere these idiots aren't hanging on our every word."

She stepped onto a ladder, motioning for me to follow her. I hesitated before descending into the dark behind her. My new human legs wobbled on each rung. Moving in the air without the support of the water made me feel awkward and heavy, as though an invisible weight hung from each arm and an ice block rested on my back. Once her feet were squarely on the floor, Ragna put her good hand on my waist to brace me. The strength and warmth in her fingers made me tremble.

"I can't believe you came back," I said, carefully stepping onto a lower rung. It was slippery with seawater and spores of a green and white plant that smelled too musky to be algae. "So much has happened. I don't even know how many days it's been."

"Eighty-seven," she breathed. "And a half. I'd have come back sooner… but I couldn't come alone."

When I reached the bottom, I turned to her. It was warmer in the ship's belly, but the air was still crisp. Our bodies pressed together, and the rough fabric of her overcoat almost made me yelp as it brushed tender new skin. Ragna's hand moved from my waist to my hips and slid under the fur she'd given me. Her other arm slipped around my back. I let the fur fall from my shoulders and embraced the cold air.

Ragna pushed me back, then tossed her coat and sword to the side. Unable to keep my balance on my new legs, I stumbled into a pile of sacks and soft material. I barely had time to look up before she pounced on top of me.

She straddled my hips, pinning me in place like an artic fox holding its prey. Smiling with sly cunning, she raised her hooked hand to her throat. Slicing a perfect line from clavicle to navel, she sliced the tunic down the middle. I caught my first glimpse of the blue-tattooed flesh beneath. Then she peeled the ruined shirt from her form and tossed it across the floor. My jaw went slack. Even when we'd struggled to stay warm together under her makeshift boat, I had never seen so much of her.

Her skin was pale and translucent around her collarbones. The tattoos ran across her breasts and stomach; the lines on her torso were more delicate than the continents on her arms. A circular compass was etched above her heart; the inky needle quivered.

When I was in my mermaid form, my scales protected me, keeping my vital organs safe from attack. I looked at my own fragile body, then up into Ragna's feral eyes. Despite their wildness, a sun-warm kindness lit their depths, a tenderness that seemed at odds with the scars on her arms and the sharp hook that had taken the place of her once-gentle hand.

I trusted her with this vulnerable body: maybe it was the animal's instincts that had come with my monstrous form, but something inside me knew that I was safe. She'd saved me from the polar bear and she'd come back, unwilling to leave me to whatever fate she'd imagined that I would suffer.

She looked into my eyes. I wrapped my arms around her back and pulled her to me.

"How did you know where to find me?" I whispered against her neck.

She grinned and glanced at the dancing lines twisting across her naked body. "I can always find what I want."

Ragna lowered her head to my neck. The edges of her teeth grazed my skin, not hard enough to break through the fragile boundary, but I felt the pressure, the controlled sharpness. She brushed her lips across mine, and I strained to kiss her. I remembered the addictive taste of her. But she just laughed, pushed me back, and grinned as she pinned me with an elbow.

Kissing and nibbling, her lips moved down my new body. A soft tangle of matted, sea-blasted hair trailed across my skin behind her kisses.

Stroking the outside of my thigh, Ragna gave me a lazy, cocky smile. I raised my eyebrow, and she propped herself up on one arm and looked right into my eyes. "I'm going to show you what your human body can do."

AS MY BREATHING EVENED OUT, I heard Ragna's throaty chuckle against my hip. I looked down at her, and she licked her lips, then smacked them together suggestively. I blushed and looked away. This kind of sex was not something the merfolk engaged in, but I couldn't pretend it hadn't been wonderful.

She watched me in the dim light, then slowly propped herself up. "Will you show me your kraken form again?"

I tensed, and the tingling happiness that had swelled inside me vanished as my heart pounded. "Why would you want to see that? It's awful."

She shrugged and held up her hook. "Do you think this is awful?"

"No." I sat up too, and took the hook in my hands. "It's just different. You were wounded. I understand."

"When I arrived on shore, my boat was almost in ruins. For days, I didn't think I was going to make it." She stroked the skin of my shoulder lazily as she spoke. "But then I washed up near a village, and an old woman helped me from the sea. She was a fisherwoman, and her husband had been killed by the men who took me."

I rested my head against her back and listened as she told her tale.

"She helped me get fit again. Fed me with everything she had and introduced to me the town blacksmith, who helped me to make some weapons. They all saw my tattoos and they knew what I was, but that wasn't why they helped. They wanted revenge as much as I did. Their village was in ruins. They just didn't know what to do."

She picked at one of the sacks beneath us and sighed. "I rested as long as I could. Then, I packed my things and I got a job at the lord's castle. The guards are eager to help a pretty girl." She made a face, and I gave a nervous little giggle. "When I got close enough to the lord, I killed him. He was fast though, faster than I expected."

"He took your hand."

She nodded. "He was fast as a crocodile with a blade. I could have chosen simply to bind the wound and let the stump heal. But I wanted to remember the fisherwoman who rescued me from the sea."

Loki had said that they left me with my monster's form to remind me. Perhaps they meant to remind me of their wrath and my own stupidity, but it could remind me of something else as well—of how I'd changed and eventually triumphed.

I lifted the vial and spoke against the glass. My body shifted immediately, and I closed my eyes, wincing at the sensation of my slimy flesh against Ragna's soft back. I pulled my tentacles back and balled myself into the corner.

"Touch me with them," she commanded.

I opened my eyes and stared at her.

"I don't want to be afraid of any part of you," she whispered, holding her bronze hook up to the light. "Touch me with them."

Releasing whatever tenuous hold I had on the tentacles, I let them splay. My legs slid over her back and hips, down her thighs and across her breasts. Ragna whimpered with something like pleasure. I hated the legs a little less.

When I had touched every inch of her, I shifted back into my human form. Ragna lay back against the sacks, sighing as her eyes drifted shut. I curled myself around her and draped her fur over both of us.

Five

I WAS DRIFTING IN THE haze between pleasure and sleep, barely aware of my surroundings or the encroaching cold nipping at my exposed human legs, when Ragna hoisted herself up. She pressed a kiss to my forehead. Squinting through half-closed eyes, I watched as she dressed. She secured her blade at her belt before making the climb back up the ladder.

I let myself pretend to sleep for a minute or two longer and drew a length of plush white fur from the sacks to wrap around my shivering body. The skin looked as though it had come from a miniature polar bear. The texture was wrong, though: spongy and thick, a cross between netting and a mermaid's hair. I scooped a few more of the skins from the bags and fashioned a cape and tunic for myself. Then I pulled the discarded brown fur on top of it all. To the sailors on the deck, I would probably look like yet another creature from the horrors of myth, but at least I was warm.

With none of Ragna's swift grace, I clambered to my feet and up the ladder. Her crew huddled in small groups. Some played with dice and coins while others crouched around fires built atop pyres of stone, cooking meat from animals I'd never seen. Even in my new human form, the smell of burning flesh made my stomach churn. I covered my nose with the edge of the brown fur. Ragna stood by the ship's prow. She was talking with the largest human I had seen. She pointed across the ice field and moved her finger as if tracing a line through the perilous ice for the ship to follow.

Catching my eye, she stopped her conversation and strode to me, her boots drumming across the deck. Most of the crew watched Ragna with a mixture of terror and awe, never daring to look her in the eye. Her remaining hand never left the exposed hilt of her silver sword. She had rolled up her sleeves, and the blue ink of her magical tattoos shifted ever so slightly. The lines of the map seemed to move in time with the ship's gentle sway, almost as if they continuously adjusted based on the changing winds and tides.

Whatever had happened to her in the months we had been apart, I had no doubt she had won this crew and ship by force, not with charm. She'd gotten her revenge. I couldn't help a pang of sympathy for the crew, who'd found themselves entangled in the web her of vengeance. They all gave her a wide berth.

Until we talked further about what had happened after Ragna lost her hand, I couldn't know if these people deserved their fate or not. The bear of a man at the prow turned. His bulging arms were bare under a cape of white fur. He watched Ragna without fear, but the boy nearest him cringed when the giant shifted his attention.

Ragna sidled up alongside me. She brushed a strand of my hair back behind my ear. Her touch was whisper-soft. "You could have slept as long as you wanted."

"Who are all these people?" I asked, flinching from her. It bothered me that these people seemed so afraid. I had enough experience with tyrannical rulers to sympathize. "This crew. They're definitely scared of you. Did they belong to the man you killed?"

She shrugged. "This ship belonged to the man I was captured for. When I killed him, I took his crew."

"But why are they so afraid?"

"They saw me kill their old lord and captain. When I gutted him, many of them were halfway up the steps, coming to his defense." She scowled and gestured at the teenaged boy who had seemed so awed by my nakedness. "And when we set sail, his father tried to lead a mutiny. We threw him overboard."

My hand went to my mouth. "You killed him? You let him drown?"

"With a stone tied around his legs. We whipped his back to a pulp first."

"That's awful," I spluttered. She was a murderer. No wonder the crew was on edge, too scared to look into her eyes. Killing her abductor was one thing... but anyone else? Someone she'd had power over? "You're a killer. That poor boy..."

Ragna's eyes hardened, and her lips pressed into a line. "And what about you?" she demanded. "What did you do to earn your human form? To become that creature I saw crawl out of the deep? That's Loki's work. Anyone can see it."

After what we'd shared the night before, her words cut me. I could see by the flash of her eyes that she knew it, too.

"I had to," I spat. "Protecting you from Havamal didn't give me a lot of choices."

"Oh, don't make it about me." Ragna clenched her jaw. "I know you saved me, but you wanted to get away from that ice mountain before you met me. And you know, I stayed? I waited there where you left me for hours, but you never came back. So, I left. I did what I had to and I still came back for you."

Guilt felt like ice gripping my throat with a frozen hand. "I made a deal with Loki. Someone died because of me."

Ragna raised her hook to the sun. Her eyes bore into mine, daring me. "Then don't you dare judge me for doing what I had to."

"I'm trying to set it right. I can't bring her back but…"

"And I'm trying to go home!" she snarled. "I want to see if there is anything left of my people and help them if I can. And what will you do, now that you have this precious magic? Come with me? Swim south and never return? Leave your people behind?"

"No!" My hands curled into fists, and suddenly I wanted to punch her. "I'm going back to the fortress. I'm going to fix things. For everyone, not just myself."

She snorted dismissively. "Good, then maybe you're not such a coward after all. I thought that maybe you were, because of how easily you let that merman drag you away."

That wasn't fair, not after the things I'd done for her on the ice shelf. My knuckles collided with her cheek. She stepped back, pressing her hand to the place where I'd struck. Behind us, several members of the crew gasped. I started to apologize, but suddenly my head snapped back, so violently it seemed my neck would break.

Cursing, Ragna shook out her fingers. My jaw burned, and pain radiated up through my teeth. We glared at each other; hostility crackled in the air. Finally, Ragna let out a slow breath. "There's something a little monstrous in both of us. And maybe it has to be that way for us to survive."

I spat a mouthful of blood over the ship's edge into the ocean. She was right. We had both done terrible things in the name of freedom and survival. But monsters or not, both of us wanted to fix our broken communities. Ragna was following her heart's navigation back to me, then to the charred ruins of her home.

My home was ruined in a different way, held hostage by a cruel false king. We would need human fire to free the princess, Loki had said, and Havamal had brought me straight to the only human who might help. Without guidance from the merfolk, the treacherous ice trap might claim Ragna's ship as she tried to get home, despite her skill as a navigator. We all needed each other.

"Gods," Ragna swore, but all the venom in her voice had vanished. She wiped a trail of blood from my lip. Blushing, she looked at the deck. "Your teeth are red. I shouldn't have hit you."

"I hit you first." I cranked my jaw to loosen it. "I won't do that again. I have enough enemies. I'm still exiled from the ice mountain. Plus, you punch better than me."

The hunter's smile appeared on Ragna's face, and she bared her teeth. Clapping me on the back, she said, "Let's see what we can do about that."

I gave her a bloody smile.

WHEN I CLIMBED OVER THE bow late that evening and scuttled down the side of the ship, Havamal waited for me. He grimaced at the sight of my tentacles, but said nothing when I folded my arms over my chest and chose to remain in the monster's form after I'd descended. If he and I were going to be friends again, I wanted him to get used to me as I was, not as he imagined I should be.

"She has what we need," I said, hovering in the water beside him. "A black substance that burns hundreds of times hotter than our scales."

As we broke our fast with strange human food, I'd told Ragna about the princess and the king's prison. In front of her entire crew, she'd wheeled out a keg filled with a thick black liquid that smelled of decay. While I watched, a hesitant archer had coated an arrow with the tar and loosed it onto the ice shelf. Despite the water and cold, the arrow had burned until the ice melted beneath it and the point fell into the sea. Even against ice thickened and reinforced over years, her fire would work.

Havamal nodded. "I went back to the glacier and I told everyone who is with us to get ready." He pulled a woven satchel over his shoulder and drew out a block of ice, wrapped with precision in flattened kelp leaves. He pressed it into my hand. "Rala carved this. It shows the north point, and he's indicated where he saw the king go."

I unwrapped the leaves and pulled out a crude statue the size of my hand. Rala had carved it in the rough shape of the point and etched a faint circle around the left corner of the berg. I turned it over in my hands and stared. I'd been so afraid to live even a part of my life locked in the glacier's heart; what would years of total solitude have done to Inkeri? If we managed to free her, would she be fit to rule?

"You're not sure, are you?" Havamal asked. He scrutinized my face, analyzing my hesitation. He squeezed my shoulder. "We have support. Truly, Erie, when you left after your trial… it was like a catalyst. Things in the glacier haven't been stable since. Even the king is nervous. He senses something isn't right, even though he doesn't understand what it is."

"The fire will work. But…" My voice trailed off. "What if we free her, and she can't lead?"

Havamal shrugged. "There are others who could help her, but we have to do this. We have to expose him and show everyone that he is a liar."

"So what?" Panic rose inside me, and for a heartbeat I wondered if I should have done what I planned all along, and simply swum away after I gained my freedom from the trickster. Deposing the king left us with a responsibility. "We just… get rid of him and hope for the best? That's the plan? These are people's lives!"

Strong arms wrapped around my back, and Havamal crushed me against his chest. My tentacles flailed in protest, but I clamped down on their instincts and forced them to be still. It was pleasant to trust him again, even if I would never depend on him in quite the same way I had when we were young. I'd learned that I was stronger than that.

"If it goes wrong, blame me," he said. "Blame me for everything if you want. I know I blame myself."

The same guilt I felt, which twisted my stomach into knots, dripped from his voice. He exhaled sharply and sent a stream of bubbles to the surface. "I wish we could plan everything down to the last detail, but we won't know how to work with Inkeri until we see her. Anyone has to be better than Calder, though."

"Will you be able to convince him to go with you?" I asked. "To the bay, when it's time?"

Havamal nodded. "He trusts me again. It took him a while, but he thinks my intentions about making you my mate were good. Plus, he will never turn down the chance to hunt blue tuna."

I ran my fingers across the row of missing scales on his stomach. His hand found the exposed patch on my back. We'd suffered enough at the king's hands, directed by his cruel laws. Everyone in the glacier had endured his maliciousness for too long, and it was time to take our freedom back.

Six

I RODE ON THE SHIP with Ragna and stood at the prow alongside
her second in command as the crew rowed the vessel into the bay.
Ragna paced back and forth. A line of tar barrels stood ready on
the deck, and the crew's two archers had their arrows nocked.

"I hope you know what you're doing," the huge mountain of
a man said, rubbing the beard at his chin. "This bay is dangerous,
and if we hit the ice…"

He didn't have to say it. I knew what the icebergs did to ships.

The man shook his head slowly as he watched Ragna pace.
"The crew resents her, but she cares for them. She would blame
herself if anything happened."

I nodded, knowing how that felt.

"That man she told you about," the big man hesitated and
rubbed the back of his head, stealing a glance toward Ragna as if
to confirm she couldn't hear him. "The one we threw overboard.
She didn't tell you he slit a night sentry's throat and tried to dump
the water supply in the ocean in order to further his mutiny. He
was a bad egg who would have killed us all to get what he wanted.
The rest of the crew will come around."

I didn't know why Ragna's lieutenant chose to tell me about the man she'd killed, but when I looked at her again, something in me softened.

We coasted into the bay, and I studied the north point. The ice mountain was twice the size of our fortress, with sharp ledges and high peaks. Its sides were so slippery that no land animals made their home atop it. Even the polar bears were afraid of the mountain. It was the perfect place for the king to have hidden Inkeri for all these years.

Using signs and sketches, Havamal had drawn more information from Rala. They had already scouted the area. Although they couldn't see the princess, Havamal had found a long shaft under the water where food could be lowered. Ragna's archers would have to aim for the ice above. Then we would somehow have to get the princess out through the fissure.

I swallowed, praying hard that Ragna's men were as good with weapons as she was. The operation was becoming too complicated, with too many opportunities for things to go wrong. Part of me wanted to tell Ragna to turn the ship around. Then we could sail away together, and I could see the world as I'd always wanted to. But if I left, everyone Havamal brought with him would be at the mercy of the king. If he thought Havamal had betrayed him, Calder wouldn't stop at cutting out his tongue. If I turned around now, I would be the same coward I'd been before Loki entrapped me, thinking only of myself.

Ragna directed the ship to the other side of the north point. When Havamal lured King Calder to the bay, I wanted the human ship to be out of sight. If the king grew suspicious, he could flee to the safety of the glacier and those who supported him.

Havamal had said there were plenty who were on our side, but were afraid. Without the princess, how many would back Havamal?

As we drew closer to the glacier, I crawled over the edge of the bow. Using the suction in my tentacles, I balanced on the side of the ship right above the water. From this vantage point, I'd be able to see the ice under the waves and signal Ragna. The ice had claimed many ships, ripping their hulls apart with its jagged underwater peaks. We wanted to hide in the shadow of the glacier without sinking the boat.

On the deck, I heard Ragna's boots drumming as she continued to pace. I wondered if she'd chosen the pair to sound imposing. Given the image she seemed to want to project to her men, such a conscious choice wouldn't surprise me.

The ship turned the final corner, hugging tight to the berg. For the first time, I really surveyed the craft. Where the whaling ships coasted low in the water, this ship skimmed the surface, as agile on the waves as a porpoise. It passed easily over the sharp ice, and the oarsmen stopped their furious rowing as someone dropped a heavy anchor into the ocean. I nearly fell as the ship heaved back when the anchor's chain forced it to stop.

Ragna's face appeared over the ledge. She leaned down, and I climbed just high enough to brush my hand against hers.

"You'll be ready for my signal?" I asked.

She nodded, then beckoned to me. I pulled myself up alongside her. Her fingers dug into my hair and yanked my face to hers. "In case you don't make it back."

A sob welled in me, and I fought to keep it down. If she kissed me, I knew I would cry, so as Ragna lowered her lips to mine,

I sank my teeth into her neck. I didn't break the skin, but she yelped nonetheless and stood up.

"What was that for? I mean, I admit, under another circumstance and accompanying…" she blushed and trailed off. "Is that a mermaid thing?"

I smirked, arming myself with a bravado I didn't feel. "Now we have unfinished business. So I have to come back."

I didn't wait for her to argue. Instead, I pushed off the ship with all my strength and dove into the sea.

I ATTACHED MYSELF TO THE underside of the point and waited in the dark for Havamal and the rest of King Calder's hunting party to appear. A pair of great white sharks swam laps around the iceberg's base, rooting in the crevices for fish. The bolder of the two sharks approached me. He swished his tail and looked at the strong tentacles that kept me attached to the glacier like a turquoise barnacle while he tasted the water for my smell.

When I crept closer, the shark spooked and darted away. I almost laughed. The great whites inspired terror across the ocean. What did it say about me that I scared them?

I clutched Loki's vial. I'd gotten so used to murmuring the invocation that the words had become a blur, almost without meaning. The trickster hadn't reappeared, and I supposed they were giving me space, hoping the misery of our deals faded in my memory so they could compel me to work with them. What was a few days to a god who lived for millennia? I made a silent promise, a prayer, not to Loki or any of the other gods watching from Asgard, but to myself. I was through living a life driven by others. I would never get involved with the trickster again, no matter how desperate I became.

A pale blue light flickered in the dimness: Havamal's signal. I could picture the jellyfish he held in his hand, illuminating the way toward a mythical school of tuna as he bought time and trust by chattering to the king about feasts and parties and pretty mermaids. I moved to the edge of the iceberg before whispering the invocation and shifting into my new mermaid form.

I swam out to greet the hunting party, plastering my best smile in place. My new pearl scales glittered, and I arranged my hair so it half covered my face.

"I'm lost," I called, making a show of swimming sideways as if I were confused and starving, struggling to stay upright. "Please, I'm lost."

"Whoa," Calder breathed as he caught the flicker of my multicolored tail. I moved my hips suggestively. He turned to his companions and whooped. "Have you ever seen such a beautiful creature? She must be a long, long way from home. What are you doing here, my starfish?"

His use of the silly nickname made me want to vomit. But I forced myself to simper and swim a few feet toward him. He would see what he wanted to see.

"Bet she's fertile," said a yellow-finned guard by the king's right arm. Calder licked his lips and passed the man his whalebone trident. His look of possession made my stomach squirm. Pure lust was dulling the king's instincts and killing all traces of suspicion... for the moment. But, if this plan didn't work, and these animals attacked me, I hoped I would be able to defend myself. I prayed that giving me the vial hadn't been a trick of

Loki's. I could imagine the trickster retracting my abilities at exactly the moment that would leave me the most vulnerable.

There was a murmur of assent from a few of the guards, but those with Havamal formed a circle around Calder's back. He was too enraptured by my strange and beautiful scales, too used to the guards circling around him, to notice as the hunting party split into factions. Havamal still held the jellyfish light, but he made no move to close the gap between us. I stayed half hidden in the shadows.

I molded my features into an innocent, wide-eyed expression. I pulled more of my hair across my face and peered through the curtain of blue. "Where am I?"

Calder swam toward me with an expression of wonder on his face. Up close, all the pockmarks and scratches on his weathered skin stood out. I'd always thought of the king as a handsome man, but maybe the cruelty inside him was beginning to show on the outside. He adjusted the mother-of-pearl crown that rested atop his head and extended his hand to me.

I closed my eyes and shifted forms, as I pivoted to gain speed. My tentacles fanned around me, whipping into the king's remaining loyal guards as I spun. I knocked them aside as if they were toys. The lust in Calder's green eyes darkened to fear. In a flash of silver light, Havamal swam up behind him. He pressed the end of his tapered harpoon to the back of the king's neck.

"Traitor," Calder hissed, his voice as low as an eel's rasp. "Traitors, all of you. Siding with this fugitive? She's a killer and, from the looks of her new powers, she's sold her soul again."

"Quiet," Havamal said, jabbing the harpoon. A trickle of blood flowed from the king's neck, then diffused in the water.

I wondered if the white sharks would come back and finish the king for us.

King Calder swallowed hard, but his chin remained raised, defiant.

"It's interesting you bring up treason," Havamal drawled. I had to respect him for his control. His voice didn't betray anger, and the rest of the guards took their cue from him, remaining silent and still, with their arms crossed. He really had grown up. "We are here to prove treason was committed. A long time ago."

Only three of the assembled hunting party had remained loyal to the king. The three guards bobbed in the water now, rendered unconscious by the blows from my legs. At Havamal's nod, one of the men with us swam to check their breathing. He rested two fingers beneath each sagging chin and pronounced each alive in turn.

Havamal beckoned to me, and I swam from the glacier's shadow into the open water. His men trembled, tightening their circle around Havamal to put distance between themselves and my muscular tentacles. Sighing, I shifted back into mermaid form. But the beautiful scales that had drawn looks of appreciation only moments ago now had the men exchanging nervous looks. Magic scared them even more than the monstrosity of my legs.

Two of the men grabbed the king by both arms. Silent Rala swam forward, his eyes blazing with a lust for revenge as bright as his ruby fins. He considered his sovereign, then opened his mouth and flashed the stump of his tongue for all to see. All the color drained from the king's face as he realized what Havamal meant by treason and why we had come to the north point. Rala led us around the iceberg to the left corner where he'd marked his carving, where Ragna waited to blow the ice apart.

Rala swam to the glacier's edge and felt around with his hands. His arm sank into a tunnel. He turned to us with a triumphant smile. The king flailed in the guards' grip. He clipped the guard on his right with an elbow to the back of the head, but another guard swam to them. In seconds, the men subdued the king, wrestling his arms behind his back.

I swam for the surface, gathering as much as speed as I could. The shimmering fins Loki had given me seemed to buzz with energy and strength. I dug my nails into my palm. I couldn't think that; Loki hadn't *given* me anything. I had paid for this magic with suffering, and, despite the invocation, it belonged to me now, not the trickster god.

With a final kick, I breached into the air. The sunlight glistened on the colors in my scales like a beacon. I landed with sideways splash, signaling to Ragna that it was time.

The rest of Havamal's hunting party surfaced behind me. Most of the men kept their distance, but at their new leader's beckoning they swam a few feet closer. We waited for Ragna to move into position.

When the ship rounded the corner, positioning itself alongside the glacier, a few of the mermen gave cries of fear. But Havamal steadied them with a few quiet words. I smiled at him across the waves. It was the first real smile I'd given him since our ordeal began. He had matured so much in only a few months, had grown into a military commander other men trusted and followed—and maybe into a friend that I could trust too.

Havamal, Ragna, me… we'd all made unforgiveable mistakes. But maybe forgiveness wasn't necessary. We couldn't change what we'd done, but I hoped that today we'd create something new, something good.

When they got close enough, I could see the archers on Ragna's ship climb onto the prow. The crew rolled the barrels of tar forward. The boat groaned under the added weight, and its bow tilted toward the water.

"Aim for the crevices," Ragna shouted. "The arrows won't penetrate the ice. They need to rest on the shelves and burn."

She climbed onto the dragon's head that decorated the bow and sat atop it. The wild arctic wind made her golden hair billow behind her as if she had her own set of sails. I watched her as she screamed directions. Longing bubbled up in me. The vial's magic wasn't the only thing I wanted to claim as mine.

A flurry of flaming stars shot through the morning sky. Some missed their targets and slipped across the ice's slick surface until their flames were extinguished by the ocean waves. But bit by bit, the archers coated the surface of the ice with sticky tar that burned.

"This is crazy," the king announced, trying once again to wrench his arms free. He turned to Havamal, entreating, "Stop it. You're accomplishing nothing but allowing these humans to pollute the ocean with their toxic fire. Release me, and we can discuss this. It needn't end badly for you."

Havamal pressed his lips together and ignored his former sovereign. The ice glowed with fire, and we all waited. Then a cracking noise pierced the silence, and a section of the thick ice broke off from the glacier to hit the ocean with a mighty splash.

We all swam forward to look. Havamal swore. A great fissure had broken in the ice, but it was several feet above the waterline. Even if the guards managed to breach high enough to jump inside and look for the princess, they would never be able to crawl back out. There wouldn't be enough water inside to allow them to swim.

Calder raised a challenging eyebrow and then folded his arms stubbornly over his broad chest. "I'll see the lot of you stripped of scales and left to die. Maybe we can get some of that human fire and burn you alive. I bet that would be fun."

Pure fury erupted inside me. I wanted him to pay for the system he'd created, for the princess he'd abused, for all the mermaids living in darkness, and for the sake of his prideful power that angered the gods and made them curse us. In a flash, I shifted into the monster's form and climbed up the ice. I knew it could be dangerous to go inside alone. After the fire had burned away the surface, the glacier would be unstable. I'd lived inside the ice long enough to know how unpredictable it could be. The walls around the prison might collapse and kill both the princess and me. Worse yet, what if I was trapped down there with her, a prisoner?

Without pausing to think further, I shifted forms. I didn't let fear stop me as I plunged into the fissure. Instinct positioned each of my legs exactly where it needed to be, bracing my body by sticking to both sides of the slick ice tunnel. I descended lower and lower into the ice, until water touched my scales. Diving into pure darkness, I stretched out my hand.

And someone grabbed it.

Keeping hold of Loki's talisman in my left hand, I hauled the princess up with my right. It shouldn't have been so easy to lift her outside the water. I peered at her, squinting to see her against the blue gloom. She was a skeleton with a shriveled body, her flesh stretched too tightly over her bones. Her limp green hair clung to her head in patches and her emerald tail was riddled with open sores.

She held onto my hand with all the strength she still possessed. She'd spent years sealed in this ice prison, all alone. It would have been easy for her to resign herself to her fate and let death take her. Inkeri wanted to survive and she wasn't about to give up now.

But as I pulled her up and positioned her on my back, my grip on Loki's vial slipped. The little bottle fell from my hand and was swallowed by shadow. My heart nearly stopped. I needed to get the princess to safety, but the fissure wasn't stable. The outside wall of the north point had partially crumbled as a result of the fire. The tunnel I'd crawled through could close at any time, leaving both of us sealed within the dark chamber. But if I left the bottle behind, I might be stuck in this monstrous body forever.

I reached down with one of my tentacles, desperately feeling about in a space I couldn't see. A piece of ice the size of a seal pup broke off in the tunnel and fell toward us. I ducked, and the princess let out a hoarse scream as the crystal boulder narrowly missed her face. If I didn't pull us to safety, we would die here. And not only us. Havamal would die. The other mermen who had helped us would die, too.

Blood pounded in my ears. I'd be stuck in a monster's form, feared by my own kind, an outcast, and unable to lie with Ragna intimately ever again, even if she accepted me as I was. I shut my eyes against the hot tears. Perhaps this was fate's punishment for Vigdis. I swallowed hard and climbed for the opening that led to the sky.

I would wear this monster's form, but I didn't want a monster's heart.

ANOTHER CHUNK OF ICE FELL down the tunnel. It scraped my face, leaving a gash that dripped blood down my chest. The princess pulled herself so tight against me that I could feel the wild beating of her heart. Each of the mouths on the underside of my tentacles burned from the cold of the ice, but I forced myself to climb until we emerged into the sun.

A cheer erupted from the crew on Ragna's ship, then from Havamal's men. I jumped off the lip of the fissure, plunging into the water below. This time when I advanced on them, none of the guards loyal to Havamal looked at me with fear. Instead, they rubbed the back of their heads, mouths agape. Despite my situation, I felt a little glow of pride. They appreciated me for something I'd done, not how I looked.

Havamal extended his hand to Inkeri. She untangled herself from my grasp and placed her fragile hand in his. Havamal lifted the pale fingers to his lips and kissed them; his eyes never left Inkeri's face. "My lady. It's an honor."

I almost laughed at his formality until I noticed the change in Inkeri's expression. The corners of her lips twitched, and then a smile blossomed, lighting up her tired eyes. Havamal gestured to his guards. One by one, the men folded in graceful bows. The princess straightened, lifting her chin as their reverence gave her confidence. She needed this respect to help restore her as the queen she should have been.

"Kidnapping!" The king shouted, turning to his former guards with wild eyes. He looked at Inkeri, but didn't seem to be able to address her. Maybe he had some sense of shame after all. Instead, he looked past the princess as if she didn't exist to beseech Havamal, "Someone has kidnapped my sister and put her here all these years—"

"Silence," Inkeri ordered, her voice shaky with disuse. She steadied herself on Havamal's offered arm before continuing. "You poisoned me to keep me weak and sick, and when that failed, you brought me here and left me to rot, feeding me only enough to keep me alive so Aegir wouldn't feel my death."

The mermen gasped. The three who had been loyal to the king had roused in my absence, and even they looked at their sovereign with murder in their eyes.

Calder struggled, but the men held him. Snarling at his sister, he spat, "You were weak and useless. You could have never been a strong ruler."

"No," she said, looking from guard to guard, then back to her brother. "But maybe I'll be a good one."

A smile twitched at my lips. In the light of the open water, the damage to her body was even more shocking. Her bones jutted at odd angles, as if they had been broken and healed badly. The green of her scales had worn to leathery brown. She looked as though her body, starved of the sun and warmth, had already started to rot in her ice grave. But the strength of her words told me she would recover, and she would lead. And the way Havamal looked at her, as if she were a miracle despite the condition of her body, told me that he would help her, if only as a form of penance.

Havamal plucked the pearl crown from the king's head and set it on Inkeri's. She smiled as she adjusted it atop her patchwork hair. Then she turned to me. My heart leapt into my mouth as she held out a golden vial. "I think you dropped this."

I wanted to sink onto the ice before her. I wanted to throw myself at her and kiss her. Relief made my body light and my head dizzy. I took the little vial and pressed it to my chest. My fingers trembled. "Thank you."

She blinked at me. Her lashes were long, her eyes deep cerulean. She might be beautiful again, given time. "No, thank you. For whatever you had to do to achieve this."

The princess took a firmer grip on Havamal's arm. He gave her another half bow, then blushed all the way to his ears. "Half the glacier already knows," he said. "They are waiting, and the others won't support him once they see evidence of what he's done."

Inkeri nodded. Her eyes hardened when she looked at her brother. I saw the former king swallow hard.

"You should just let us gut him right here," one of the guards grunted. "We could strip his scales off and give him to the humans. Let them turn him into soup. Or fry him up. They deserve something for their help, after all."

The king went pale. He looked at his sister, then closed his eyes and bowed his head. The fight drained out of him. He was at the mercy of the girl he'd tortured for over a decade and he knew it.

"We'll have a proper trial," Inkeri said, brushing what remained of her hair back from her face. "I don't want to start my rule as a tyrant. I don't want to hide any of the details of what he's done."

The guards murmured their assent, and Havamal squeezed Inkeri's arm a little tighter. I suppressed a smile. Something told me that Havamal might get his happiness after all.

"What about you?" Havamal asked, peeling his eyes off Inkeri long enough to turn to me. "Are you coming back with us?"

With a new ruler, the glacier community could put itself back together. The people could establish new laws and customs. Girls who had feared years of dank imprisonment would be free to dream again. Maybe the clan would move to a new home in warmer waters. Inkeri would need time to recover her physical strength, but her mind was still sharp, and I knew she could trust Havamal to be her support and her friend, as he'd once been for me.

I let the smile I'd been holding back blossom. It was the first time I'd been able to think about the bond Havamal and I had shared without a trace of pain. I wouldn't begrudge either of them if he transferred his affection to the queen.

I wanted to see what my home would become. But if I stayed, Loki would always know where to find me, and I'd never get to see the world or live out my own dreams. Even if my home changed, my desire to see everything had not. With my new forms, I could see everything, go everywhere. I still had that burning wanderlust. Only now, it didn't seem so selfish.

When I could, I'd return to see what they'd built together.

I looked up to the surface of the water, where the dark shadow of Ragna's ship's hull hovered above us. "Someday," I said. Then, after Havamal took a deep breath and anxiety clouded his eyes, I amended. "Someday soon. But first, I have to help someone else get home."

Epilogue

THE SALT AND WIND WHIPPED through my hair as I dangled off the ship's bow. A green coast loomed ahead, framed by jagged rocks and a beach of sparkling sand. Flowers bloomed across the landscape. Trees taller than our mast dotted the hills beyond, and a flock of miniature polar bears grazed beneath them, bleating to one another. After a lifetime spent in the monochromatic world of the arctic, the riot of color nearly stole my breath.

Ragna rode the dragon's head behind me; a smile spread wide across her face.

"Look at that farmland!" A jubilant boy's voice shouted from above. "Have you ever seen somewhere so green?"

I took Ragna's hand and gave it a little squeeze. For the past few days, she'd been growing more and more restless, waiting for the sight of land. I had spent nearly every waking moment above deck, taking in sights and smells I'd never imagined, relishing the might of the waves and the beauty of the ship that could take us anywhere.

Ragna tilted her face to the wind as she took in the smell of the coast and the blast of fresh air. Her cheeks were flushed, and her eyes were brighter than I'd ever seen them. Ocean spray washed over us as the ship crested over a frothing wave. Even the sea felt better here, where the salt in the water was diluted by frequent rain. The spray was a familiar caress against my wind-chapped skin. She kissed the top my hair. I sighed with pleasure and rested against her knees.

The freedom of the open ocean embraced us.

What we had might not be forever, but it was now, and it was everything I needed.

THE END

Acknowledgments

First, I want to thank my partners, my family, and my friends for putting up with me during the crazy, busy year that has been 2016. I've missed or cancelled a lot of plans in order to write or edit. Thank you for your support, your understanding, and your love. I know I'm not always easy.

The Seafarer's Kiss was the work of a small village. It started as the kernel of an idea that transformed into a short story, then a novelette, then went on submission, before being reined back in by my amazing bookish friends and readers, who insisted it become a novel. I'm so glad you insisted.

Thank You:

To Nina Rossing, Jessica Gunn, and Carrie DiRisio, who read the rough passages and talked with me about this book from the very beginning.

To Katherine Locke, for taking an uneven first draft, insisting it had potential, and helping me whip it into shape with tact and brilliance.

To EM Castellan, Ava Jae, Marieke Nijkamp, Laura Lam, and CM Lloyd who offered invaluable feedback while this book was in progress.

To the Interlude Press team, especially Annie Harper, for taking the book of my heart and making it truly magical.

About the Author

JULIA IS A POLYAMOROUS, BISEXUAL writer and native of Chicago who now resides in Edinburgh, Scotland, where she spends her days enmeshed in the book trade and her nights penning fantasy novels. Julia has been an avid traveler since childhood; her explorations inspire the worlds she creates. Her first novel, *Unicorn Tracks*, was published by Harmony Ink Press in 2016.

The Seafarer's Kiss was influenced by her postgraduate work in medieval literature at The University of St. Andrews. It is also responsible for her total obsession with beluga whales.

an imprint of interlude**press**

@duet**books**

Twitter | Tumblr

For a reader's guide to **The Seafarer's Kiss** *and book club prompts, please visit duetbooks.com.*